Home Court Advantage

Sandra Diersch

James Lorimer & Company Ltd., Publishers
Toronto, 2001

James Lorimer & Company Ltd. acknowledges the support of the
Ontario Arts Council. We acknowledge the support of the
Government of Canada through the Book Publishing Industry
Development Program (BPIDP) for our publishing activities. We
acknowledge the support of the Canada Council for the Arts for
our publishing program.

Cover illustration: Greg Ruhl

Cataloguing in Publication Data

Diersch, Sandra
   Home court advantage

(Sports stories; 51)
ISBN 1-55028-749-4 (bound)   ISBN 1-55028-748-6 (pbk.)

I. Title. II. Series: Sports stories (Toronto, Ont); 51.

PS8557.I385H64 2001   jC813'.54   C2001-901227-6
PZ7.D57338Ho 2001

James Lorimer & Company Ltd.,	Distributed in the United States by:
Publishers	Orca Book Publishers
35 Britain Street	P.O. Box 468
Toronto, Ontario	Custer, WA USA
M5A 1R7	98240–0468
www.lorimer.ca	

Printed and bound in Canada.

Contents

For my brother, Adam,
who found his forever family a long time ago
and for all the waiting children and parents
who have yet to find each other.

Special thanks to Joan, Jon and Rebecca
for sharing their expertise with me
and to Dustin, Josh, Keaton
and the students of division two at
Yennadon Elementary School
for their suggestions and comments.

1

Traveling

Debbie received the pass from her best friend, Jenna, and stood for a second, bouncing the ball slowly, weighing her options. She changed hands and took a step to the left, then back again, then to the right. She grinned at the group gathered in front of her, waiting to pounce as soon as she moved, and threaded the ball through her legs. Then she bolted straight up court, gaining the foul line before most of the other kids realized she had moved. She laid in an easy two-pointer and turned to accept the cheering and hand-slapping from her teammates.

"You traveled," Jamie Scudamore told her, her face red from running, and ugly from the scowl she wore.

Debbie ignored her. What if she had traveled? She would have scored regardless. She always scored. The other kids always wanted her on their team when they played at recess or lunch.

"You traveled," Jamie repeated.

"Get lost, Jamie. You're just sore because your team is losing. You're sore because you didn't get me for your team."

"I wouldn't want you on my team. You cheat, you smell bad and you're stupid."

"Jamie is a dumb jerk and you know it. Don't let her get to you — you know you're the one who'll get in trouble." The voice spoke slow and steady in her head as she ran up and down the court.

After Jenna missed a lay-up, the other team raced up-court. One of Jamie's friends got the ball at the side and threw a poor shot that hit the rim and bounced into the hands of a forward. Debbie, thinking she might get a fast break, turned and raced back toward her own basket. The pass wasn't long enough and Debbie had to slow down to catch it. When she pivoted to shoot, Jamie ran in to block her. When Debbie threw up an unbalanced shot, they collided and fell, Debbie landing in a heap on top of the other girl. She grinned as she got to her feet, dusting off the seat of her faded jeans.

Jenna caught the tip off and dribbled down the side slowly, her head up. Debbie caught her eye from the middle of the court, but Jenna shook her head. There were too many opponents around her. Frustrated, Debbie charged left, then quickly back up the middle, losing a couple of kids in the process. Jenna passed her the ball and she turned. Jamie appeared in front of her, arms outstretched, challenging her as Debbie tried to set up to pass to a teammate. Debbie turned her back on the girl, her body curled around the ball protectively, then she faked right, went left and turned, throwing the ball as she did. As her arms came down from the throw her elbow hit something hard and she turned around to see Jamie leaning over, her hands covering her face.

"You alright?" she asked, but Jamie didn't answer. "Ah, she's fine," Debbie said at last, shaking her head. "She's just faking it to hold up the game. I hardly hit her."

"Let's play," someone called, bouncing the ball restlessly.

"She broke my nose, the stupid cow!" Jamie cried, raising her head finally. Her nose was bleeding a little and there were tears in her eyes. "Where are the supervisors?" she asked, looking around. A drop of blood fell from her nose and hit the pavement.

"It isn't broken." Debbie shook her head, panic rising in her. Her track record was poor. Would the supervisors believe her when she said she hadn't done anything on purpose? It was hard to know. "I hardly bumped you."

Jamie glared at Debbie, hatred in her eyes. "You shouldn't be allowed to play with us," Jamie said at last. "You should be tied to a supervisor's leg at lunch!"

Debbie cringed at the words. The anger was rising in her, bubbling nearer and nearer the surface. She knew she should walk away. That was what the counselor had told her over and over. Just walk away when kids start saying things to upset you. But her feet felt planted to the ground. The only thing moving was her hands as they balled into two tight fists at her sides. Then she felt Jenna beside her.

"Why don't we head back," Jenna said in a soft voice. "The bell's going to ring any second anyway."

Debbie nodded, shooting a fierce glare at Jamie and her friend as she and Jenna left the court together.

"Did you study for that socials test?" Jenna asked as they rounded the corner and were out of sight of the other girls. Debbie had relaxed again, the anger mostly gone.

"There's a socials test?"

"Oh, Debbie. Didn't you study? You're really going to catch it from Ms. Westerman this time."

"No big deal. I can fake it," she said, hating the pitying tone in her friend's voice. Jenna had probably studied half the night for this thing.

Debbie kicked at a loose piece of pavement outside the classroom as they waited for Ms. Westerman to open the door. She found her house key in her pocket and played with it. Who cared about some stupid socials test anyway? She'd rather play basketball. And it was hard to study at the Barkers, her foster family, with a seven- and nine-year-old running around playing Star Wars with their light sabers and sound effects. Jenna didn't say anything else, but the look she gave Debbie made her uncomfortable.

"I'll just copy off your test," she said, teasing, but Jenna didn't laugh.

Once inside the class, Debbie hung up her coat and went to her desk. She slouched in her chair, acting as uncaring as she could manage. All the other kids had their books out and were rereading notes but Debbie just stared hard at the top of her desk, scowling. It was going to be a long hour.

* * *

"What's going on this afternoon, dance?" Debbie asked as she and Jenna walked home together at the end of the day. Her foster brother and sister, Jason and Nadine, trailed along behind, dragging their bags in the dirt and bickering at each other, like they did every day.

"No, Guides after dinner. We have to talk about the camp we're going to in a few weeks."

Debbie stared enviously at her friend. Guides and camps. Whole weekends sleeping in sleeping bags and eating marshmallows cooked over a campfire, singing songs with other girls; it all sounded amazing. Once, when Debbie had been eight, she had gone camping with her first foster family, Carrie and David McKenzie. They had pitched a tent and built a fire and fished for their dinner. It had been great. The Barkers never camped. They weren't the camping type, according to Darlene.

"I wish I could go to a camp with you sometime," Debbie said with a sigh.

"I don't understand why you won't just ask Darlene to let you join Guides. My mom would take you to the meetings."

"Yeah, maybe I will someday," Debbie said, but she knew she would never ask Darlene to let her join Guides. She was pretty sure the answer would be no, and she just didn't want to hear it. Foster kids didn't get to join clubs and take lessons. Those things were for kids with real parents, like Jenna.

"Hurry up, Nadine, Darlene said you had to get home quick today," Debbie nagged at the little girl, who had stopped to try and entice a cat out from behind a bush.

"I just want to pat the kitten," the seven-year-old said, advancing on the cat.

"If you fall in the ditch," Debbie told her, "your mother is going to freak and she's going to blame me. And if she blames me, I definitely won't play Barbies with you next time you ask."

"You're mean, Debbie," Nadine told her, moving away from the cat.

"No, I'm just older than you." She grinned at Jenna, who shook her head, trying not to laugh.

"You wanna stop for a while and shoot some hoops?" Debbie asked, pausing at the end of the driveway. Nadine and Jason ran for the house and disappeared inside.

"I'd like to, Deb," Jenna said, "but Mom said to come right home. Homework."

"Right," Debbie agreed, like she knew exactly what Jenna was talking about. "Maybe another time then."

"I'll see you tomorrow, right? Eight o'clock? Don't forget to finish that book report tonight!" Jenna called with a wave as she continued down the road.

Debbie watched her go, feeling a little abandoned. Jenna was a great friend, but she was so busy all the time. She hardly had time after school to just hang out and goof around. When Jenna had disappeared around the corner, Debbie picked up her nearly empty backpack and let herself into the house.

The old house was big and drafty with most of the bedrooms, the kitchen, living room, and dining room all upstairs. Debbie's room was downstairs with the unfinished family room and the washer and dryer. She had her own bathroom, though, which Jenna said was a good thing. Still, it was kind of lonely down there, all by herself. The kids didn't play downstairs because the room was unfinished and Darlene only came down to do the laundry once a week. Steve kept saying he was going to finish the walls and Darlene was going to paint, but so far it hadn't happened.

"You home, Debbie?" Darlene called down the stairs.

"Yeah!"

"Come up here for a second, would you?"

Nadine and Jason were sitting at the table eating when Debbie came into the kitchen. Her own stomach started grumbling and she reached for one of the cookies on the plate.

"Hey! Now the number's wrong," Jason complained, crumbs falling from his mouth as he spoke.

"So?"

"Don't cause a problem, Debbie," Darlene told her. "Debbie will get another cookie, Jason, don't worry."

"What's going on?" Debbie asked as she handed Jason a cookie and took one for herself.

"I have to take Nadine to the dentist," Darlene said, frowning at the list in her hand. At the table, Nadine made a face. Debbie nodded in agreement. She hated going to the dentist too. "And Jason needs a haircut, badly. I also have some errands to run and we're going to stop at my mother's to pick something up. Would you please stay here and start dinner? Nadine has Brownies at six-thirty tonight and we're going to be pressed for time. And Leanne called and wants to come by tonight. She's coming at seven."

"Leanne is coming? Why?"

"She didn't say why, just that it was important that she come tonight. Okay, guys, let's get going, we have tons to do. Don't forget dinner, Debbie."

Debbie watched out the front room window as the minivan backed out of the long driveway. She would have liked to visit Darlene's mother, who was pretty cool and always treated her like she was another grandchild. But what was her social worker coming for? Debbie couldn't figure that out at all.

2

Some Kind of Mistake

Time seemed to go very slowly that afternoon. Debbie stared for a while at her school books, but got next to nothing done. Then she went outside with her basketball and shot some hoops, but her mind kept wandering and she kept missing. There weren't a lot of reasons she could think of that would bring her social worker out for an unscheduled visit in the middle of the week. Unless she was going to be moved again. Leanne had shown up unexpectedly when David and Carrie had told her they wouldn't be her foster parents anymore. Was that what was happening this time? A chill went down Debbie's back.

Didn't Darlene and Steve want her anymore? she wondered, trying to remember something she had done wrong recently. Or maybe, like David and Carrie, they were being transferred, or maybe Darlene was pregnant. Debbie closed her eyes and sat on the stone steps at the side of the driveway. She didn't want to go to another foster home. She wanted to stay with the Barkers.

Leanne arrived just as Darlene returned from taking Nadine to Brownies. Steve joined them, and the three adults and Debbie sat in the living room together. Debbie held her hands tightly between her knees, waiting for the ax to fall.

"I got a call from another social worker yesterday, phoning on behalf of clients of hers who are interested in meeting

Debbie with the possibility of adopting her," Leanne said, coming straight to the point.

The world seemed to stand still, the air didn't move, Debbie didn't blink or breathe or even twitch. The words hung in the silent, still air, growing larger, as though being blown up like a balloon. They loomed before Debbie, until she almost shrank back in fear. How long had she waited to hear those words? Seven years. Ever since she knew her mother wasn't coming back to get her.

"Debbie? Are you okay?" Leanne asked, leaning forward to touch her knee. "I know this comes as a bit of a shock. I was shocked too. To be honest, it is unusual for a child your age to be placed, but it does happen. And it seems it could happen to you. Would you like to know more?"

Silently Debbie nodded. She wanted to know if these people had seen a picture of her. If they knew she wasn't cute and little and blonde. That she wasn't six. Were they insane? Nuts? Stupid?

"Their names are Greg and Angela Lowell and they live in Maple Ridge. Greg is a high school teacher and Angie gives piano lessons. They've been married for almost fifteen years and have no children of their own."

"And they want to adopt Debbie?" Steve asked.

"Yes."

"Well, Debbie, this is quite something for you. Aren't you going to say anything?" Darlene asked.

"I think Debbie is a little overwhelmed," Leanne said gently, smiling. "I'm going to leave you now, to think about all this. Angie and Greg would like to meet you as soon as it can be arranged. They're quite excited."

"Have they seen a picture of me?" Debbie finally managed to ask.

How could they possibly want her when there were tons of cute little girls who didn't get into fights at school, who didn't get suspended, who were interested in dresses and dances and music lessons. What if they met her and realized it had all been a horrible mistake? What if they met her and then changed their minds?

"Debbie, I want you to know that before I ever mentioned this to you, Greg and Angie had spent hours with their social worker looking over case files of different children available to be adopted. They are very, very adamant that they want an older child. And they want a girl. They saw your picture and read your file. I talked to them for a long time about you. They know about your family situation and how many times you've been moved. They know all about you. I can't lie to you and say there isn't a chance that things could fall through, that the adoption could not take place in the end, but Debbie, it doesn't happen very often. We take great care to prevent that kind of thing. I don't want you to be hurt any more than you want to be hurt. Do you understand what I'm saying? You're the last to know this. They want to meet you. Can I arrange a time?"

"They know all about me?" Debbie asked.

"Yes."

"And they want to meet me anyway?"

"Yes."

"Am I allowed to say no way if I don't like them?"

"Yes."

"Okay, I'll meet them."

* * *

The restaurant was crowded with lunch customers when Leanne and Debbie pushed their way through the doors the following Saturday. It had been a long week, waiting. What were they like? They knew all about her, but Debbie knew very little about either of them: their names, where they lived and what they did for a living, that was it. Big deal. How come she didn't get a file on them? There had to be one. Leanne had probably read it. Debbie trusted Leanne more than she trusted most people and Leanne seemed pretty sure about this whole thing. But Debbie was finding it hard to believe.

"I think they're already here, Deb," Leanne told her, smiling at the hostess and heading for the back of the restaurant. "I know you're nervous," she whispered, taking Debbie's hand and squeezing it. "But you are not on trial here. If anything, Greg and Angie are, because they're terrified you won't like them. So just be yourself, okay? And no decisions are being made today. This is just a first meeting."

Debbie nodded, scanning the back of the restaurant carefully. She spotted them, finally, sitting in the very last booth in the corner. Nice and private in case the foster kid lost it or something, she guessed. She assumed that the two people sitting close together on one side of the table were Angie and Greg. They looked young. Too young to want someone as old as Debbie. The other woman, sitting on a chair that had been placed at the end of the booth and was blocking traffic, must be their social worker.

"Here they are!" the woman said, brightly, jumping to her feet as Leanne and Debbie arrived at the table. "Hi, Leanne, good to see you again. And this must be Debbie. Hi, Debbie. I'm Rhonda. And this is Greg and Angie Lowell."

Debbie turned from the overly enthusiastic Rhonda to the people who thought they wanted to be her parents. Greg grinned, his brown eyes crinkling up under bushy eyebrows. He had a small, neat brown beard with just a hint of grey in it and lots of wavy brown hair on the top of his head. The hand that shook hers was warm and strong. Angie had short blonde hair and startlingly blue eyes. Her smile showed small, perfect white teeth.

"We are so glad to finally meet you, Debbie," she said, her voice quavering just a little. Was she going to cry or get mushy? Debbie wondered. She hoped not. She hated crying.

"Yes, it feels like we've known you for ages, just from your photos and what we've read about you," Greg added, still grinning. "Not that words capture a person completely, though, eh?" He chuckled, then stopped when no one else joined in.

"This is Leanne Phillips," Rhonda said, continuing the introductions, "Debbie's social worker."

There was more hand-shaking and finally Debbie and Leanne were sitting down with menus in front of them. Debbie was suddenly starving. She hadn't been able to eat breakfast and now everything on the menu sounded amazing.

"You must be thinking this whole deal is kind of one-sided, eh Debbie?" Greg asked once the waitress had taken their orders. "I mean, we know a lot more about you than you know about us."

"Yes," Angie agreed. "You must have so many questions. We're prepared to answer them, so ask away."

"Why do you want to adopt someone as old as me? Everyone always wants the little kids."

"I told you she'd ask the toughest one first," Angie said to Greg, her smile never leaving Debbie. "We weren't able to have children of our own, Debbie," she explained. "And by the time we were ready to consider adopting, we knew we didn't really want a baby anymore. We like our jobs, and we like traveling and taking off at the drop of a hat for ski weekends or whatever. Greg is busy at school after hours and on weekends sometimes. All our nieces and nephews are older; the youngest is nine, and our friends' kids are getting older too. Having a baby now would be a lot more work and inconvenience than we were prepared for. Plus, it's very difficult to adopt a baby."

"So," Greg continued, squeezing his wife's hand, "we took the ages of all our nieces and nephews and friends' kids and averaged them and ended up with eleven."

Angie laughed and swatted him gently on the shoulder. "That wasn't how we decided on an age, Debbie. Really, we just decided we wanted a girl between the ages of eight and thirteen and we liked you the best of all the kids whose files we looked at. Simple as that."

The waitress arrived with their food and for several minutes there was the usual chaotic clatter of cutlery and moving plates while they all started eating their meals. Debbie had noticed that Greg's lunch was meatless. Would he expect her to be a vegetarian too? She wouldn't, no way, she thought as she bit into her dripping hamburger.

"Was that your only question?" Greg asked when they'd had a chance to eat for a while.

"What do you teach at the high school?"

"I teach history and coach the boy's basketball team," Greg told her with a twinkle in his eyes.

Debbie shivered as though she had suddenly grown cold. Basketball? Was this some kind of joke? "Really?" she asked.

"You bet. I understand you're quite the basketball player yourself."

Debbie shrugged and stuffed some fries in her mouth. She looked at Greg again, chewing slowly. He was still grinning at her. "Is that why you chose me?" It was a dumb reason, she thought, for choosing a kid to adopt. Why not choose someone who looked kind of like you? Or who was smart and cute? Why choose a dummy just because she could throw hoops?

"It was one of a whole bunch of reasons, Debbie," Angie said.

"What were some of the others then?"

"You've always wanted a dog," Angie told her.

"And we have one of those," Greg added.

"Leanne thinks you'd do best as an only child and we don't plan on adding any more kids to our family."

Debbie watched them both as they went down their list, trading reasons back and forth. It was like shopping for a house or something, she thought. This is the list of features we want, now find us a kid who matches up. She squirmed uncomfortably and reached for her root beer.

"Then there's the name thing, Ang," Greg reminded his wife. He looked at Debbie, a smile playing at his lips, and said, "My middle name is Deborah."

Debbie snorted, pop spraying out her nose. She covered her mouth with her hand as Leanne passed her a serviette. She looked at Greg, then, and they smiled at each other across the cluttered table.

3

Doubts

Debbie, have you got your reading assignment ready to hand in?" Ms. Westerman asked Monday morning. Debbie blinked up at her, confused. "The assignment, Debbie. It's due today. Do you have it ready to hand in?"

"Yeah, it's around here someplace," Debbie said, pawing through the mess of papers in her zippered binder. She found the slightly crinkled papers with the pencil drawing of Pegasus the Winged Horse on the front cover and handed it to the teacher, not meeting her eyes.

"Thank you," Ms. Westerman said and moved away.

Ever since the lunch on Saturday, Debbie's thoughts had been swirling. For every good thing about Greg and Angie she imagined something bad. Yes, the house was right across the street from the school, but what if she hated the teacher? Yes, Greg taught basketball, but what if he was mean? He didn't seem mean, but he could have been putting on an act. And they were so pushy. That very night everyone was meeting at a restaurant somewhere for dinner so Greg and Angie could meet the Barkers.

"Pull out your novels and let's have a look at the next chapter," Ms. Westerman said.

Debbie pulled her book out of her desk and opened it to the right page. Maybe she should call and ask Leanne about some of this stuff.

"This is going to be very confusing and a little overwhelming for you, Debbie," Leanne had said in the car on Saturday. "I expect there will be lots of questions and worries popping into your head. Any time you need to talk, you can call me."

"Yeah, sure, okay," Debbie had agreed. But her brain had been blank then. Or not blank, really, but so full of the lunch and the things they'd said and just seeing two people who might be her mom and dad very soon that she couldn't think of a single question. Not until she'd gone to bed that night. Then she'd started coming up with all these problems.

Like how would Darlene and Steve feel? They'd taken care of her for nearly three years, and at the first hint of something better, Debbie wanted to take off. They'd said they were thrilled for her to have the chance at a real family, but what if they were lying?

"Debbie," Ms. Westerman said, a hint of impatience in her voice. She must have said it a couple of times, Debbie thought as she looked up. "Would you please read the next paragraph?"

"Page fifty-one, third paragraph down," Jenna hissed.

Debbie read awkwardly through the paragraph then tuned out again, thinking instead of her questions. Leanne had suggested that she make a list of questions as they came to her, that way, when she saw the Lowells or Leanne, she could remember them better. She slipped a piece of paper out of her binder and hid it behind the novel. With a quick glance at the teacher, she wrote;

   1) Can I visit Jenna any time I want?
   2) Can I change my mind after they adopt me and go back to Darlene and Steve?
   3) Can Angie and Greg change their minds?
   4) What if I don't like the house or the school?
   5) Do I have to be a vegetarian like Greg?
   6) Can I be a Girl Guide?
   7) Can I still see Leanne sometimes?

"Psst, Deb," Jenna whispered, "Ms. Westerman is watching you. You'd better get to work."

Debbie nodded and slipped the paper into her desk, then pulled her notebook toward her and started on the questions. What would she do without Jenna? she wondered.

* * *

Somehow Debbie got through the dinner that night. Jason and Nadine managed to behave themselves and no one said or did anything embarrassing, but at the end of the evening, Leanne dropped another surprise.

"That wasn't so bad, was it?" she asked when they were momentarily alone. Debbie shrugged. She didn't want to talk about it, didn't want to think about it.

"Greg and Angie will be coming to the house on Thursday night and we're going to sit down, all of us, and talk about you."

Debbie went cold. "Me? Why do you want to talk about me? What are you going to talk about?"

"Everything. Darlene and Steve are going to tell the Lowells all about you, your habits and likes and dislikes, everything they can think of. And you are too."

"Are you trying to scare them away?" It sounded awful to Debbie. Why did they have to do that? No one wanted to know that she took showers that were way too long and then left wet towels lying on the bathroom floor. They didn't want to know that she hated cauliflower and corn and that she had a habit of sneaking cookies out of the bag.

"Not at all! We're trying to get rid of surprises, Debbie. Don't you want Angie and Greg to know who you are? Darlene and Steve do, don't they? Bad habits don't make people like or dislike someone. We all have them. They aren't going to change their minds because you forget to put the cap on the toothpaste."

Leanne smiled, but Debbie couldn't. Would Darlene tell about the time Debbie had "borrowed" the loose change from their dresser? Or about when she'd forgotten to pay for the candy at the corner store? What about how she sometimes screamed in the middle of the night, great horrifying screams that woke everyone in the whole house except Debbie? Would they tell Angie and Greg about the fights she sometimes got into at school?

"It's okay, Deb, I promise. Nothing that will be said is going to change the Lowells' minds. I know all about you and I still like you, don't I? And I'll be there."

"It's all going so fast," Debbie said, her head spinning.

"Yes, it does go quickly. Angie and Greg are eager to have you come to their home for good, if that's your decision. They've been waiting a long time for a daughter."

"Well, they can come, but I can't promise that anyone will behave themselves."

* * *

Debbie rushed home from school Thursday afternoon and spent an hour cleaning her room; making the bed, picking clothes up off the floor, putting garbage in the bin. She even vacuumed and wiped down her bathroom. If they were going to hear all the rotten things about her (Leanne had said there would be lots of good things to share, like how she was teaching Nadine to play basketball, but Debbie wasn't sure if the good would outweigh the bad) then she would try and cushion it all by being neat and tidy. She would even put on her best clothes.

Debbie hardly ate any dinner, waiting for the Lowells to arrive. At a quarter to seven, Debbie went outside into the November evening with her basketball and waited, looking restlessly up and down the quiet, shadowy street. Questions ran through her head with each bounce of the orange ball. No answers, just endless questions:

8) Can I visit with Darlene and Steve sometimes?

9) Where will I spend Christmas?

10) Do they know that I have a bad temper?

She was so immersed in her questions and in trying to perfect some tricky footwork that she didn't hear the car drive up or Greg and Angie come up behind her until Greg startled her by applauding when she sank a basket. She flushed as she turned around.

"Well," she said, cradling the basketball against her chest like armour, "let's get this over with." Then she turned, without waiting for Greg or Angie, and went into the house.

But they didn't start right in, ripping Debbie apart. The adults all sat in the living room, drinking coffee and chatting while Debbie sat in a chair in the corner, feeling like she was waiting to be executed. Finally Angie looked over and smiled at her.

"I'd really like to see your room. Would you show me around a little?" she asked, standing up.

Reluctantly, Debbie nodded. "I guess. There isn't much to see, though."

"That's okay."

Downstairs, away from the others, Angie's smile relaxed and she let out a breath. "That's tough, isn't it?" she said, her voice low, conspiratorial. "I have to admit I'm really nervous."

Debbie glanced at her, curious. Why was she nervous? It was Debbie they were going to talk about, expose to the world for the horrible child she was.

"This is my room. And that's my own bathroom," she said, not responding to Angie's comment.

"Wow. Aren't you lucky having your own private suite like this! I would have killed for a bathroom of my own when I was your age. I had to share with two brothers and a sister."

"Well, Nadine sometimes comes down and uses the bathtub."

Debbie sat on the edge of the poorly made bed and watched as Angie moved around the room. She was pretty, Debbie decided finally. Her short hair was blonde and hung straight to her chin. Her eyes were blue and she had little freckles running across her nose. She turned suddenly while Debbie was staring at her, and Debbie blushed.

"This must be very overwhelming for you." Angie sat down on the chair by the desk and clasped her hands. "I know I've been feeling that way myself."

Debbie shrugged and picked at the fabric of the bedspread.

"Is this your class photo?" Angie asked, picking up a frame from the desk.

"Last year's."

"Oh, there you are! Your hair was longer then. Which one of these girls is your friend Jenna?" Angie asked.

"The girl sitting beside me."

"I hope I'll get a chance to meet her."

"Why?"

"Well, because she's important in your life. And meeting the people you're close to helps me to know you a bit better. Like meeting Darlene and Steve."

"I'm nothing special, you know," Debbie said, her chin jutting out a little. "I don't play the piano or sing or dance. I've never been in a club or on a team or anything. I don't know how to cook and I'm really bad at math. Isn't that what you're here for tonight? To hear all that stuff?"

"Yes, partly. But you know, we aren't looking for a perfect child. You certainly won't be getting perfect parents in us. Besides, I happen to think that the good outweighs the bad in your case."

"We should go back upstairs," Debbie said abruptly, standing and moving to the door. If they were going to spill all her nasty little secrets, she figured it was better just to get it over with.

4

The Speeding Train

Debbie reached into her lunch bag and pulled out the bag of carrots. She made a face and tried again. An apple. Where was the good stuff? When the bag was empty, the contents sitting on the top of Debbie's desk, she shook her head in disgust. She was not going to let Darlene make her lunches anymore. Debbie packed much more interesting stuff when she made lunch for herself.

"Aren't you going to eat?" Jenna asked.

"There isn't anything worth eating," Debbie told her, crunching on a carrot stick reluctantly.

"I bet Angie won't let you eat the stuff you always eat either, you know."

"Shut up. I can eat what I want."

Jenna laughed. "I bet you'll end up being a vegetarian like Greg before Easter," she teased.

"I'm not going to tell you things if you're just going to make fun of me." Debbie picked up the tuna sandwich and bit into it. Then she took another bite. She was really hungry. They'd had gym just before lunch and Ms. Westerman had worked them hard.

"Oh, don't be stupid about it. When do you see them again?" Jenna asked.

There had been lots of visits since that first Saturday, including that night when Greg and Angie had come over and they'd all sat around the table in the dining room and talked about her. It had felt like hours and hours, but it hadn't really been that long. And Debbie had been surprised. Darlene had told Greg and Angie about the loose change and the shoplifting and the fighting and the most amazing thing had happened.

Greg, who was sitting beside Debbie, had taken her hand and held it. He'd smiled at her. "First I want to tell you that when I was ten I 'borrowed' change from my dad for months. He could never figure out why he never had any. And I never confessed and offered to pay it all back like you did. Second, we already knew all about that. We already knew all of this. Nothing that was said tonight was new to us."

Debbie stared at him, confused. "You already knew?"

"Yes," Angie said, nodding. "It's in your file, Debbie. All of the good stuff too, like how generous you are and how kind you are to animals. The point is, we wanted you to know that we knew it all. All about the warts as well as the dimples, as my Gran used to say."

"And you still want to adopt me?" She couldn't quite believe that could be true.

"We still want to adopt you."

She knew they were waiting for her to say that she would let them. They were all waiting for that. And she would. But not just yet. First she needed to see the house, the school, meet their dog, Poker, and see her room. Then she'd know for sure.

Debbie grinned at Jenna across their desks. "They're coming here, to school, this Friday afternoon. They want to meet you and Ms. Westerman and see the school and stuff."

"Really? Are you nervous?"

"Yeah. They're going to talk to the principal too, and look at my report cards and my file. And then I'm going to their place for the weekend. The whole weekend. And Angie will bring me back to school Monday morning."

Jenna finished her apple and threw the core in the garbage. "That's pretty fast," she said, sounding sad. "Will they let you and me visit sometimes, do you think?"

"Definitely. I asked Greg and he said anytime."

Debbie had shown them her list, and Angie and Greg had gone through and answered every question, right there on the page beside Debbie's scratchy handwriting.

"Are you finished eating?" Jenna asked, standing over Debbie's desk, a basketball tucked under her arm. Debbie nodded and stood up, tossing the remainder of her lunch in the garbage. "Then let's play."

* * *

It was very strange, waking up in a room in a house where she might live forever. There had been quite a few beds over the years, but none of them had ever felt like hers. Would this one? she wondered. She lay in bed for a few minutes, listening to the strange sounds around her. The day before had passed in a blur. She hardly remembered meeting Greg and Angie at the office at school, introducing them to the principal, to Ms. Westerman and to Jenna, showing them her desk and classroom. And then, before she knew it, she was in the car and they were driving out to Maple Ridge. She did remember meeting Poker. All red and white fur and licking tongue and wagging tail, he had practically knocked her over when she'd come in the front door. Debbie hadn't minded, though, she thought, petting the sleeping dog who lay beside her on the bed. So far Poker was the best thing. Well, him and the basketball hoop sunk in cement at the side of the driveway.

Angie made pancakes for breakfast, which was the first uncomfortable thing, because Debbie hated pancakes. She stared at the small round cakes sitting on her plate, and then at the arrangement of syrups and jams on the little spinning tray on the table in front of her. Her hands held tightly between her knees, her stomach grumbling fiercely, Debbie tried to talk herself into trying the food.

"Is something wrong, Debbie?" Angie asked, appearing at her side. She held a dishtowel in one hand and kept running the other hand down the length of it, over and over and over. "Don't you like pancakes?"

"Not really," Debbie whispered, heat rushing to her face.

Greg, who was halfway through his first plateful, pointed his fork at her, looking serious. "I'll bet you've never tasted pancakes as good as Angie's," he said.

The only pancakes Debbie could remember eating were Darlene's: hard, tasteless rocks that sat in the bottom of her stomach for the rest of the day, making her feel like she was going to throw up at any second. She eyed Angie's pancakes suspiciously. Greg certainly seemed to be enjoying himself. He popped another forkful in his mouth and chewed elaborately, rolling his eyes and groaning. Debbie tried not to smile at his obvious acting. Angie was still standing beside Debbie. Debbie could feel her and wished she'd go away. She made her nervous.

Reluctantly Debbie picked up her fork and knife and cut a small piece from one pancake. There was nothing wrong with these pancakes, she discovered quickly. "They're pretty good, I guess," she admitted. Angie grinned and went back to the griddle. Debbie exchanged glances with Greg.

"Told you so. I'll bet you're used to pancakes that sink to the bottom of your stomach, right? Like Angie's sister, Beth. Beth makes the lousiest pancakes on the face of the earth," Greg said.

"Greg," Angie said in a warning voice.

"Well she does!" He winked at Debbie. "But I promise you something, Debbie, if you come here to live forever, you will not be disappointed in the meals. My wife is an amazing cook."

Debbie finished the pancakes on her plate and when Angie came over offering seconds, she held her plate out eagerly, smiling shyly at Angie. "Thanks," she mumbled.

When they'd finished eating and Debbie had helped Greg with the cleaning up, she went up to her room. She stood in the doorway looking in at the guest room. None of the furniture matched — the headboard was white but the dresser was painted yellow. The bedside table was plain wood with a small lamp on it. In the corner was a rocker with an old quilt thrown over it. There were pictures on the walls but Debbie didn't like any of them. She didn't like the room at all.

Angie had promised that by the time she moved in during Christmas holidays, the room would be painted and there would be new furniture. They would go shopping together and pick it out. Debbie already knew what she wanted. She'd seen a picture of a bedroom set: bed, dresser, desk and bedside table, in a magazine ad. All of it was in a warm, honey-coloured wood. And she wanted the walls to be purple, pale purple.

Debbie quickly made the bed, not bothering to smooth the wrinkles or fluff the pillows. She brushed her teeth and ran a comb through her hair and then pulled her books from her backpack. Angie had suggested Debbie work on her homework while she taught her lessons and Greg did some of his own work. There was homework. There was always homework: two pages of math, questions for a story, a socials project that was due before Christmas. But what was the point? She was probably going to move here to Maple Ridge over Christmas anyway. Why bother with work now?

She looked out the window for a while at the big backyard and the houses across the lane. There were dogs in three of them, that she could see. And there was Poker, below her, sniffing at a bush in the corner. He had gone out first thing and was still out there. Greg said he spent most of his time outside. He was a hunting dog and hunting dogs liked to be outside, sniffing out the little birds that hid in the shrubs and trees.

Debbie heard a door open below her and the sound of unfamiliar voices, then Angie laughed. Her student, Debbie guessed. Angie had shown Debbie her music studio last night. It had its own entrance, with a small waiting room where the students waited their turn and then the larger room with the piano, a keyboard, shelves of music books and the computer with its own printer. There were pictures of composers on the walls and little lesson cards too, like what Ms. Westerman had in the classroom, teaching what a quarter note was and a treble clef. Debbie knew about those from music at school. But they had only learned to play the stupid recorder and to sing really dumb songs.

After a while Debbie went downstairs. She found her jacket in the closet and her shoes on the shoe rack in the garage, found the basketball and headed outside. It was grey and cool out but dry. The Lowells' driveway wasn't as long as the Barker's and the hoop was set at the side of the pavement, not over the garage. It took Debbie a couple of minutes to get used to the difference. She couldn't run full out down the length of the driveway and do a jump shot the way she could at home, so she practiced her free throws instead. She wished Jenna was there with her. They had been practicing free throws during lunch the previous week. Jenna was convinced they'd both make the team in January.

Debbie let the ball drop through the hoop and roll away onto the road, struck by a sudden, horrifying thought. She wouldn't be around for try-outs in January! She'd be here, right here in this driveway, without Jenna. Was there a basketball team here in Maple Ridge, at the school she could see across the street? Were they any good? What if there wasn't a team?

"Is this your ball?"

Debbie turned, still frowning, wondering about the whole business, doubting her decision, to see a girl about her own age standing at the end of the driveway, a basketball cradled in her arms. Her red hair was tied back in a scruffy pony tail and there was a smudge on her cheek.

"It just rolled across the road and onto our grass. Is it yours?"

"I guess. Thanks."

"You one of Angie's nieces?" the girl asked. Nosy, Debbie thought.

"No."

"Because Angie and Greg have tons of nieces and nephews. There's always some kids over here visiting. Greg and Angie couldn't have their own kids. I think they're gonna adopt some kid now or something. My mom wasn't sure. She thought she'd heard something like that."

"Can I have my ball back?" Debbie asked, her voice rough. Who was this red-headed girl with her big mouth? What did she know about anything?

"Sure," the girl said, bouncing it across the pavement toward Debbie. She didn't leave though, as Debbie had thought she would. "Do you play?" she asked instead, indicating the hoop with a dirty finger.

"Some."

"Because my brother Scott plays. Greg's his teacher, or coach I guess. Scott says he's pretty good, as far as coaches go. You staying here all weekend?"

Debbie nodded, her eyes focused on the orange ball dropping from her fingertips. She liked how it kept coming back to the exact same spot, like there was an elastic band attached to her fingers, pulling it back each time. She put as little pressure on the ball as she could, trying to see how far she could go before the ball wouldn't bounce back up.

"What's your name? I'm Paige Arnold. You can ask Greg about Scott Arnold. He plays guard for the high school team. Greg is always saying how good Scott is. Maybe he'll play in university. He's not sure. Are you any good?"

"I'm pretty good," she said, shrugging. She was very good, but why was it any of this girl's business anyway? This Paige Arnold.

"Debbie, could you come inside please?" Angie called from the front door. She waved when she noticed Paige at the end of the driveway. "Hi Paige. How's your dad doing? Is he over that surgery yet?"

"Hi, Angie. Dad's fine. He's out in the garden planting bulbs. Mom's inside having a fit. I was just returning the ball to Debbie."

"That was nice of you. Tell your mother I said hello. Debbie?"

Debbie headed for the house, relieved to be pulled away from the nosy, chatty Paige. Still, she had been friendly and she looked like she was in Debbie's grade. But she asked too many questions! Questions that were none of her business. Still, at least now Debbie knew one person in this new neighbourhood, and, since she'd decided that morning over breakfast that she would like to be adopted by Greg and Angie, that would be a good thing. She hung up her coat and put her shoes away, then went to find Angie.

5

Final Days

G et your junk off my desk," Debbie snapped on a wet Monday morning two weeks before the holidays.

Her desk was very near the coat hooks and this wasn't the first time someone had used it as a resting spot for their belongings. She glared at Jamie. Jamie had done it on purpose, Debbie was sure, just to make her angry. It didn't take much to make her angry these days, either. She wasn't sleeping very well and woke up tired and irritable most mornings.

"Chill out, Debbie."

"I said, get your junk off my desk," Debbie repeated, sweeping the pile of books and papers off her desk and onto the floor.

"You witch!" Jamie screamed. "What are you doing!" She shoved Debbie, who had to take a step back to keep from falling.

"Keep your filthy hands to yourself!" Debbie advanced toward Jamie, hands out, ready to attack whatever body part was closest.

"You're crazy! Do you know that? Crazy!"

Debbie lunged at the other girl and Jamie ended up on the floor, Debbie on top of her. She held on tight, swearing under her breath.

"What is going on in here! Girls! Stop it!"

Debbie heard the teacher's voice, felt the arms reaching to grab her from on top of Jamie, smelled the faint hint of blood from where she'd scratched her own hand on Jamie's zipper, but everything was clouded over by the anger she could taste. She hated Jamie Scudamore. Hated her. The thought ran through her head like a chant as the teacher led her down the hall to the principal's office.

"Sit there and don't say or do anything, understand?" the teacher, someone Debbie recognized but couldn't name, told her firmly. She fell into the chair in the office, scowling. It took a couple of minutes for her to realize that she was alone. Jamie hadn't been dragged down here, just her. Figured! She was always, always the only one punished, the only one blamed. No one ever stood up and said it wasn't Debbie's fault. She glared at the closed door of the principal's office. Of course, she'd take her time too, make Debbie sit out here where every little punk kid could see her, laugh at her.

"Come in here please, Debbie," the principal said from the door to her office, finally. She stood aside to let Debbie pass, then closed the door behind her.

* * *

A few dry days made the basketball court more appealing after days and days of rain and cold, and on Thursday, Debbie, Jenna and some others from their class gathered at lunch to play. Debbie had always hated inside days. There was never anything much to do and more often than not she ended up in trouble of some kind. After the incident with Jamie she had gotten into trouble for bothering some grade threes and then she was kicked out of the library for drawing little stick figures on the tables. They would have washed off, it was only pencil, but no, the librarian had to have a cow and Debbie was banned from the library until after the holidays.

Debbie didn't care, she wasn't going to be in this stupid school after Christmas break anyway. In the class no one but

Jenna and Ms. Westerman knew and only some of the other teachers. Greg and Angie had requested that it not be made too public. And besides, it wasn't anyone else's business.

But it was wonderful to be outside on the court, with the ball in her hands, the smell of rubber in her nostrils, the air crisp and cold even with the sun. They quickly picked sides and got down to the game.

The centre for the other team took the tap, dribbled to the left and then passed to a teammate. She dribbled toward the net, paused at the top of the key, found Debbie blocking her way and passed back to the centre. The girl broke fast for the basket, went up and collided hard with Jenna. Jenna cringed and rubbed her arm.

"You okay?" Debbie asked.

Jenna nodded, with a bit of a grimace. "Fine," she said, "let's play."

The other team grabbed the throw in and passed it down-court. Jamie bounced the ball and passed it overhead to a teammate, trying to work it closer to the basket. Then, without warning, the girl turned and pivoted, took a jump shot and got it in.

Debbie caught the in-bound pass and dribbled toward the centre line, where she hesitated before making a no-look pass to a forward, who broke fast but was held up as a player from the other team appeared out of nowhere in front of her. She spun on her pivot foot, bounced a pass to Jenna. Jenna caught the ball and passed it off to Debbie. Debbie drove for the basket, went up and laid it in easily.

She high-fived her teammates, then ran up-court ready for the next in-bound pass. Jenna picked up the pass and dished it off to Debbie. She could feel someone behind her, feel the air move as the other girl moved her hands, prepared to block if Debbie passed. She faked a shot, then made a no-look pass to a teammate instead, who took the shot. It swooshed as it dropped through the hoop. Nothing but net!

As Jamie grabbed the ball, Debbie sprinted down-court after the play. Jamie's in-bound pass was received by a tall teammate who quickly relayed a break-out pass back to Jamie. Debbie's team was caught by surprise and Jamie laid in an easy two-pointer.

They went back and forth down the court, one side scoring and then the other. Most of the kids playing had played on the school team the year before and most of them planned to make this year's team. Debbie looked around during one of the stops in play, breathing heavily, her hair hanging in her face. She would not play basketball with these kids again after next Friday. She wouldn't ever see most of them again. Not that she would miss them much, especially not Jamie. But for the past three years she had played with and fought with and learned with all these guys. She knew them. And in three and a bit weeks she would have to start learning all about a bunch of new people. People she had never seen before, except for Paige.

The bell rang, ending the game. Debbie trailed along behind the others, suddenly angry that her whole life was going to be turned upside down. She didn't want to leave this school or the kids in her class, or even Ms. Westerman. She wanted to stay. She didn't care about Angie or Greg or Poker or about the purple bedroom waiting for her and the new name. She just wanted things to stay as they were.

Two grade-three boys stood on the pavement, directly in front of Debbie, huddled over some hockey cards. Debbie pushed through them, knocking the hockey cards flying to the mud and sending one of the boys to the ground. The other boy began to cry and before Debbie knew it there was the noon-hour supervisor, helping the kid off the ground, all the while yelling at Debbie.

"What are you thinking?" she cried, gently wiping a Canucks card clean. "They were just standing there, minding their own business. Why did you have to knock them down?"

"They were in my way," Debbie told her.

"Debbie, go in to the office and stay there please. And don't knock any more eight-year-olds down on the way."

Debbie kicked at a rock lying in the dirt and headed for the door. If she closed her eyes, would her feet find their own way to the office? she wondered. She'd been there so many times, especially in the past couple of weeks, that she was pretty sure they could.

* * *

Saturday morning she woke up in her purple room, wide awake and restless. She could tell by the silence around her that Greg and Angie were still asleep. Quietly she slid out of bed, got dressed in several layers of sweats and t-shirts and went downstairs and outside, Poker trailing along behind her. Only a little after eight, it was just light outside, but Debbie didn't care. She bounced the basketball from hand to hand, watching as Poker hunted for the squirrel that tormented his life. The squirrel, thankfully, seemed to still be sleeping, but Poker didn't stop searching.

Debbie glanced across the street at Paige's quiet, dark house. Her older brother's car was still in the driveway, so he must not have the early shift at the store he worked in. And Paige's dad, Jim, wasn't in the garden yet. He was always in the garden, Debbie had discovered in the last few weeks. Mending a fence, pulling a weed, pruning a bush. Even in December when the rest of the neighbourhood had retreated to the warmth and comfort of their houses, Jim was always outside on Saturday morning, puttering.

The house next to Greg and Angie's had pale blue siding with white trim. The owners were not big gardeners, but their little girl was really cute. Her name was Elisa and Paige babysat her sometimes. Paige had said that maybe once Debbie was all moved in, they could babysit together.

Debbie shot the ball at the net and heard the familiar pinging sound as it missed, hitting the metal rim instead. She caught the rebound and tried another lay-up. This one went in smoothly. Debbie made crowd noises and ran around the driveway, waving at the imaginary audience. One day, she told herself, she would play at GM Place. One day she'd be a point guard or a centre for the WNBA.

"Hey there," Greg said, coming around the side of the house pulling a coat on over his sweats. He perched on the stone edge of the garden and rested his arms on his knees. "Whatcha doing?"

"Not much."

"What brought you out so early on such a cold morning?" Greg asked.

"Nothing."

"I had a rough night, kept waking up. My brain is just going a hundred miles an hour right now," Greg told her casually. He picked at some weeds poking out of the partially frozen dirt. Debbie bounced the ball, not answering. "There are so many changes going on around here. And next week, man, I can hardly believe you're coming here to stay forever. I have to admit I'm a bit nervous, maybe a bit scared too. I wondered if maybe you were feeling the same way, if maybe that was why you were out here." He spoke easily, his eyes on the cracked pavement under his feet.

Debbie shot the ball again then caught it on the first bounce. It was nice to know someone else was scared. It made her feel a bit better. She shrugged and went to sit beside him. The stones were cold.

"Could I change my name?" she asked eventually. It was one of the questions that had been on her mind.

"You are changing your name, to Lowell."

"Not that name, my first name. Deborah. I want to change Deborah."

"We won't ever call you Deborah, not even when we're really mad at you."

"I wouldn't answer you if you did. Couldn't I just change it?"

"Do you mind if I ask you why?" Greg said, leaning his cheek on his hand, watching her with his kind eyes.

"My mother gave me that name," she said softly, speaking to the hole in her jeans. "And she didn't want to keep me, so I don't want to keep the name she gave me."

Greg didn't answer right away and Debbie, thinking perhaps he hadn't heard her, looked up. She was startled to see that his eyes were wet. He blinked quickly and cleared his throat, giving her an awkward grin.

"You're right, she didn't keep you. But you know she was so young herself when you were born. She tried very hard to keep you because she loved you so very much and wanted to be a good mother. Right?" Debbie shrugged. She'd heard it, she just didn't buy it. "And she asked for help for a long time and all the people around her tried to help, but it got to be too much and she didn't have very much money. And you were hungry a lot and unhappy. Your mother hated that you were unhappy and she finally decided that the very best way she could show her love for you was to give you to people who could make you happy, people who would make sure you weren't hungry. And so that's what she did."

"She could have come to see me sometimes, or given me up when I was a baby."

"Maybe. Who's to say? But she didn't, and I'm awfully glad she didn't because then you couldn't be my daughter.

And you know, Deborah was your grandmother's name. It seems a shame to get rid of it just because you're angry with your birth mom." They were silent together for a while.

"What would you change your name to?" Greg asked finally, grabbing the ball from Debbie's hands. He stood up, still looking at her, and twirled the ball on his fingertip. Debbie watched in admiration. She had never managed to do that.

"I don't know, maybe Elizabeth. I like that name."

"What if we agreed to call you Deb, a nice grown-up sounding name, and we made Elizabeth your middle name? Would that suit you?" The ball spun away from him and he chased it down, then dribbled it back to Debbie.

"Deborah Elizabeth Lowell," she said, frowning.

She caught Greg's pass and moved toward the basket slowly, her eyes on Greg. There was a part of her that still wanted to start completely fresh, all new, but sometimes, especially late at night when she couldn't sleep and the house was dark and quiet, pieces of her old life, the one with her mother, came to her. She had no photos, but she remembered a woman with long brown hair and a pretty voice. And sometimes she remembered the smell of baking, though she didn't know why. "Deborah Elizabeth Lowell," she said again, slowly. "That sounds pretty good, doesn't it?"

"It sounds beautiful. A pretty name for a pretty girl."

Debbie blushed, unsure what to do with his compliments. They never rang true in her ears. Wasn't he just saying things like that to make her like him more? She already liked him pretty well. He didn't need to butter her up so much. Still, it was kind of nice to hear it. In answer, she broke into a run and rushed for the basket, jumping up with the ball in her hand and jamming it into the hoop.

6

Saying Goodbye

The last week went by quickly, and finally it was Friday. Jenna and Debbie walked home together for the last time. They stood awkwardly at the end of the driveway, looking at each other in silence.

"Well, I guess I'll see you tomorrow afternoon," Jenna said finally, scuffing her sneaker against the gravel.

"I guess."

"Well, bye," Jenna said with a wave, and for the last time Debbie watched her walk away down the road. She waited until Jenna was out of sight before heading down the long driveway, her backpack dragging in the dust behind her.

Jenna was the first to arrive for Debbie's going away party on Saturday. She stood on the front step, wearing a pretty blue dress with long sleeves and a lacy collar. Her mom had French braided her brown hair and it hung down her back like a shiny rope. The two girls looked shyly at each other. Jenna didn't look like Jenna in that dress, just like Debbie didn't feel like Debbie in the long flowered skirt and fancy purple t-shirt Angie had picked out for her. She felt like a stranger dressed up like this.

Debbie stepped back to let her friend come through the door. Poker, who had been invited to the party as part of the family, bounced and wagged as Debbie closed the door behind Jenna.

"You're the first one here. Well, except for Greg and Angie," she added, "but they've been here since about noon and they don't count." She pulled on Poker's collar, trying to get him to behave, then gave up and let Jenna say hello.

Debbie took Jenna's coat and hung it in the closet. She didn't know what to say, although they never usually had a problem talking. It was just that all the things they used to talk about didn't seem right now, when she was about to move away and start a new life.

"This is for you," Jenna said, handing Debbie a brightly wrapped package. "But you aren't allowed to open it until you get to Angie and Greg's. Okay? Promise?"

"Sure, I guess."

"Okay."

Darlene and Angie were in the kitchen, putting little pieces of food on trays. The living room was decorated with streamers and balloons. Jason, Nadine and Greg had spent hours attaching the purple and white streamers to almost every available surface in the room. There were purple and white napkins and paper plates on the white paper tablecloth in the dining room and a big bowl of grape punch.

Jenna turned to Debbie, grinning. "You don't like purple much, do you?" she teased.

The doorbell rang again. Debbie ran down to answer the door, Poker hot on her heels. Leanne was there on the doorstep. Debbie smiled shyly at her and moved aside to let her in.

"Down, Poker!" she said sternly, grabbing at the dog's green collar.

Leanne laughed and reached down to pet the wriggling creature. "Hello, Poker. I see you got invited to the party too." She stood up and shrugged out of her coat, handing it to Debbie, who hung it in the closet.

"Well, how are you doing?" Leanne asked, touching Debbie's arm. "This is a huge day."

"I'm okay," Debbie told her, wondering if the somersaults her stomach was doing were going to result in her throwing up. She smiled weakly at Leanne.

Since Leanne had first told her about Greg and Angie, so much had happened. Sometimes Debbie had trouble taking it all in. Besides the weekend visits in Maple Ridge, she and Leanne had spent a lot of hours talking. They had talked about living at Darlene and Steve's house, about school and how hard it was for her, but mostly they had talked about this new family Debbie was going to have and how it was going to change not only Debbie's life but also Greg and Angie's. Leanne had said she felt positive Debbie was ready but sometimes, like right that second, Debbie wasn't so sure.

"Yeah? How are Greg and Angie?"

Debbie shrugged. Her soon-to-be parents had been acting weird all afternoon. "Greg hasn't stopped moving since they got here. He told me he's pretty nervous. Angie is real quiet. Maybe they're changing their minds and don't know how to say it."

Leanne smiled and shook her head. "No, they aren't changing their minds. It's just that they've been waiting a very long time for this day and now that it is here, they are a little frightened. Sometimes when you have to wait and wait for something, you find it hard to believe when it actually happens. I think you know what that's like, right?"

"Maybe, a little," Debbie admitted.

"We should go upstairs and join your party," Leanne told her. "Everyone is waiting for you. Besides, I'm hungry."

* * *

Eventually it was time to leave. All the food had been eaten, including the cake Darlene had baked that morning, all the punch was gone and the afternoon was growing dark. Debbie had packed all her clothes and belongings that morning with Darlene's help. In the end there were two big suitcases filled with everything she owned plus her pack and a garbage bag filled with boots and shoes and some other things that wouldn't fit in the suitcases. The bags, except for her pack, were already in the back of the minivan. And so when Greg stood up, and said it was really time they started heading home, there was nothing for Debbie to do but say goodbye and go with them.

Everyone stood up awkwardly and Debbie wondered if the monstrous lump that sat in her chest was what a heart attack felt like, except that she was only eleven, too young to have a heart attack. She fidgeted with the napkin she held in her hand, rolling it between her fingers until little bits fell off.

"Well, Debbie," Steve began, coming toward her, "this is it. It's time for you to go with your new parents." He hugged her tightly before pulling back to look at her, smiling. "It seems very strange to all of us that you won't ever live here with us again, that we won't have to tell you to turn out the light and go to sleep, or to come in and stop playing basketball in the driveway. We'll miss you."

"Yes, we will," Darlene agreed. She hugged Debbie too, holding her just a little tighter than Steve. She cleared her throat before she spoke again. "We all wish you well in your new home with your new family. I think you've made a really terrific choice in parents."

Debbie hated the hugging, hated the damp eyes and the voices that caught and had to be cleared. She didn't like the strange pain in her chest and the burning behind her eyes. Leanne hugged her and reminded her that they would still see each other for a little while.

Jenna was last. The two girls stood looking at each other. Debbie's lump grew and she swallowed hard. "Don't go finding a new best friend in Maple Ridge," Jenna told her.

"I won't. Don't you go being best friends with that awful Jamie," Debbie said.

"As if I could! She's so horrible!"

"You're coming for a sleep-over weekend, right? After Christmas?"

Jenna nodded. "Good luck," she said softly and gave Debbie a quick squeeze.

And then that was it. The adults shook hands and the Lowell family walked out the front door and climbed into the car. Poker sat on the seat beside Debbie, looking out the window. The bags were in the back, her backpack on the floor at her feet with Jenna's package. On the front step of the house stood Darlene, Steve, Nadine and Jason, Leanne and Jenna. They waved and waved as Greg backed the van out of the long driveway, stopped, straightened, and then drove away.

* * *

"Why don't you spend some time putting your things away and getting settled, Deb," Angie told her, standing in the doorway to the bedroom, Greg beside her. "Come find us when you're done. Okay?"

Debbie turned slowly and looked at her new parents. She was still holding her backpack. Her two suitcases were sitting on the floor beside the bed. So far it was just like any weekend visit she'd had over the past months, except that Angie wouldn't be driving her back to Delta on Monday morning. She wouldn't be going back to Delta ever, except for a visit maybe.

Wordlessly she nodded. Angie smiled at her. "We're both so thrilled that you are here to stay, finally. We're glad you're going to be our daughter," she said.

"Very glad," Greg echoed, grinning. "Welcome home."

Debbie watched them leave the room and listened as their footsteps grew fainter as they went downstairs. She stared around at her room. On one of her weekend visits she and Angie had gone to the paint store and brought home dozens of little colour cards. They had finally picked a pale purple. One wall had striped wallpaper on it and bookshelves. There was a purple comforter on the bed. The bed, desk and dresser were honey-coloured wood, just like Debbie had always imagined. The rocking chair was gone and the old dresser and the pictures Angie'd had when she was a little girl. Instead there were rock posters and two prints that Angie had picked out for her. The curtains on the window were white with tiny purple swirls on them. The small portable CD player, a gift from the Barkers, sat on the dresser. There was a small pile of CDs, too. She put one in the machine and turned up the volume.

She picked up her backpack and sat at the desk. Slowly she pulled out her notebooks and pencil case. All the work would be new to her in January when she went back to school. Greg had told her that these new teachers had her file and knew she had trouble with math. They would help. And so would Greg and Angie. They already had, a few times. She shoved some things into the desk drawer and reached back into the pack, pulling out the small flat package Jenna had given her.

Inside the wrapping was a framed picture of Debbie and Jenna, taken at Deer Lake the summer before. Their arms were around each other's shoulders and they grinned into the camera like a couple of clowns. Debbie's throat thickened and her eyes burned. She pulled the little tab at the back and set the frame on the desk, staring at it, suddenly homesick. She blinked hard several times then reached in and pulled out some loose papers.

A cold wet nose pushed itself against her hand, jolting her out of her thoughts, and she looked down to find Poker sitting beside her. He wagged his tail, his big brown eyes gazing at her. They had become quite good friends during her visits and she was very glad to see him. She reached over and smoothed the fur over his head.

"Hey, boy," she whispered, sliding off the chair to the floor beside the dog. She wrapped her arms around his neck and hugged him. "Did you want to unpack my clothes?" she asked. Poker licked her chin. "Yeah, me neither. I think maybe we'll just leave it for now, hey?"

She pushed herself to her feet then went to the closet. The racks and shelves inside weren't completely empty. Besides the trip to the paint store, Debbie and Angie had been to the mall a few times. There were new shirts and pants, some new sweaters and a track suit, two new dresses and some shoes to go with them, plus the skirt and t-shirt she was still wearing. There were even some brand new packages of socks and underwear. Debbie barely glanced at the new clothes. She pulled the two suitcases over and shoved them into the closet, pushing them both right to the back. Then she quickly closed the doors again.

* * *

By Wednesday Debbie was beginning to feel a little like she belonged in the house with Greg, Angie and Poker. On Sunday they had gone cross-country skiing all day at one of the local mountains. They were so tired and sore when they got in, they had all fallen asleep on the couch. Monday Angie and Debbie had gone Christmas shopping, coming home laden down with packages for nieces and nephews Debbie still hadn't met. Debbie had spent some of her own money on gifts for Jenna and Leanne. She had even found something for Greg.

Tuesday she had gone out shopping again with Greg to buy something for Angie. Shopping with Greg was a lot different than shopping with Angie, Debbie discovered. Angie liked to browse, taking her time in a store. Greg, however, knew exactly what he wanted. He went in, bought it and came out again. Debbie thought she liked Greg's way better, it was more efficient.

Wednesday was Angie's ensemble practice. She and three other musicians met at someone's house and played together for a couple of hours.

"I'll leave you two to get into trouble together," Angie said as she gathered her music.

"We're going to play a game of one-on-one," Debbie told her. "Although I don't know why I want to," she added to Greg as Angie drove away, "since you just beat me every time we play."

"If you think that way, then I probably will," Greg told her. "Just try and do better than the last time."

She bounced the ball to Greg and took up her position between him and the basket, leaning forward on her toes, knees bent, the way he had shown her. Her hands were up, eyes on Greg. She tried to read his mind: When would he break and run? He bounced the ball once, twice, watching her, a smile playing at his lips, then suddenly he bolted to her left. But Debbie had anticipated him, and threw herself in his way, blocking his path and stealing the ball in the process. She moved away from him, grinning to herself, protecting the ball with her body. Greg moved with her, ready to pounce. Her big problem was that she couldn't get the ball over his head the way he could over hers. She needed stilts.

Then she remembered something he had told her once: "There will always be taller players and stronger players. Use your size to your advantage." She backed up a couple of steps, then ran forward, moving to Greg's left. As he reached out to tip the ball away from her, she wheeled away and ducked under his extended arm, sinking the ball easily.

"Way to go!" he cried, giving her a high five.

Debbie grinned as she shook her head. "You're the enemy," she reminded him, "you're not supposed to cheer me when I score."

They set up again, this time with Greg in possession. This time he had anticipated her steal and stepped aside, pivoting on one foot and shooting a fade-away shot over his shoulder. It went in easily. They were tied.

It didn't take long for Greg to build a nice lead over Debbie but in the end, although she lost, again, it wasn't by nearly as much. And she didn't mind losing to him because she knew he wasn't going easy on her.

"Okay, enough," Greg said after their third game. "I've had it! I'm old, Deb, I'm breaking down."

"That's it? You're giving up? I was just getting good."

"That's the problem. You keep me running too hard. I'm used to coaching basketball, not playing."

She grinned at him and shot the ball at the net. "Fine. I'm hungry anyway."

7

Settling In

Christmas holidays passed way too quickly as far as Debbie was concerned. There was the blur of meeting all of Angie and Greg's relatives. She would have stayed hidden in her room every time someone came over, playing with the hand-held computer game she got for Christmas, except that they were all so nice to her. No one acted funny or looked at her differently. The little kids asked questions about the Barkers, but she just answered them and that was it.

The best part of the whole thing was meeting Angie's parents, Dora and Mike. Gran and Pops. It hadn't taken Debbie long to call them by their special names, not once she'd met them and spent time playing Battleships with Gran and listening to Pops tell really dumb jokes on Christmas Eve.

The very worst thing of the holidays was the fight Debbie had with Angie. Their very first one as mother and daughter, about something as silly as the state Debbie's room was in. It began on Christmas night.

When the last of the cousins had gone home, Debbie escaped to her room to lie on her bed and unwind. Poker, who had hidden under Greg's desk all afternoon, came out and lay beside her. With one hand stroking his side and the other under her head, Debbie stared at the ceiling, exhausted.

Her purple room, which had been so incredibly tidy and pretty when she had moved in the week before, looked like a disaster now. The many changes of clothes she had gone through over the last couple of days lay strewn around the room, on the bed, on the chair and hung from the closet door. The new stack of CDs she had received from Gran and Pops were lying spread across the desk and two of the many games were on the floor, open, their pieces scattered across the carpet. A plate, a glass and a napkin were on the dresser. The remains of the wrapping paper she had used to wrap the gifts she'd given were spilling out of the open closet and the garbage can was overflowing.

Angie and Greg appeared in the doorway. They looked tired too, after entertaining four kids all afternoon and getting wumped at Battleships six or seven times.

"This place is frightening," Angie said, grimacing at the mess.

Debbie glanced at them and then back at the ceiling. It was no worse than her room in Delta had ever been. She hardly noticed.

"I think, before Greg's mother and sister arrive tomorrow for brunch," Angie continued, "that this place needs to be straightened up. You don't have to do it right this second. But it does need to be done first thing tomorrow. Before anything else."

Debbie closed her eyes, envisioning herself falling asleep without having to get up and brush her teeth or wash her face, without pajamas or a last glass of milk.

"Deb? Did you hear what I said?" Angie asked.

"Yeah. Cleaning my room tomorrow."

"Good."

The next morning Debbie took Poker out for his run in the park, stopping at Paige's on the way home to say Merry Christmas and to check out all the stuff Paige had been given. When she got home Angie was busy in the kitchen preparing something that smelled wonderful. She chased Debbie away with her spoon.

"You go change your clothes and straighten your room. Then you can come down and help. Greg's mom will be here about noon."

Upstairs Debbie looked around for a second. It looked fine to her. She didn't mind the mess. Finally she tossed the game pieces and the rules back in their box and put the lid on. Then she took both games and stuck them on the shelf in the closet.

She heard Angie come up the stairs and her bedroom door close with a click. Debbie stood staring at her clothes for a while, trying to decide what to wear. The unpacked bags were still in the back of the closet but something held her back from opening them. They were her escape, should she need it. She was managing on the stuff Angie had bought. Finally she pulled out a pair of black pants and a red sweater and put those on. Then she went downstairs.

"Deb! Get up here please! Now!" Angie called seconds later. "You still haven't cleaned your room!" she cried when Debbie came up the stairs.

Debbie glanced in the room and then back at Angie. "It looks fine to me," she said.

"No, Deb, it isn't fine. There are clothes all over the furniture, toys and CDs everywhere, your bed isn't made. Greg's mother is very fussy about things. She is going to want to see your room. Is this what you want her to see? And what about Aunt Connie and Emma? Don't you want to make a good impression?"

"I don't care. It's my room and I think it looks fine. Darlene never made a big fuss about my room."

Angie's fair skin was red right up to her hairline and she took several deep breaths before answering. "What Darlene did and what Greg and I do are two entirely different things. We are your parents and I would like you to take some pride in your belongings. You painted the walls so carefully and selected each picture. How can you let it look like this now?"

Debbie shrugged. Angie made way too big a deal about things as far as she was concerned. Just because the rest of the house looked like a magazine, didn't mean Debbie's room had to.

"Here's the deal. I would like the bed made, the clothes put away properly, the gifts put away and the garbage bin emptied. I would like all those things done before you come downstairs again. Do you understand? I don't think it is too much to ask of you to keep your room looking respectable."

"You're sending me to my room?" Debbie asked, surprised.

Angie looked surprised herself. "Yes, Deb, I am. It will take you two minutes to do. So get on it."

But now the holidays were over, and school was going back in on Monday. Debbie would cross the street with Angie first thing and find her new class. Angie had told her that her teacher's name was Mr. Anderson, and had shown Debbie where the class was from the outside. But peering through the window was quite different than being in the class with twenty-five sets of eyes looking at her. Paige was in that class, though, and that was the only good thing Debbie could think of.

* * *

An empty desk was added to Paige's group at the back of the class. Debbie put her notebooks and binder on the desk and stood looking around the room. She and Paige and Mr. Anderson were the only ones in the class; the rest of the kids were still outside waiting for the bell. There were posters on the wall and displays of the kids' artwork. Mr. Anderson's desk was cleaned off. Ms. Westerman's desk had always been covered in layers of papers. Maybe this desk was clean because they were coming back from the holiday, Debbie thought. Her own desk would be a disaster by the end of the week.

"Here is a socials text and a grammar text, Debbie. We'll get you settled into a group for our novel study too, at some point. Did you already study Japan in Delta?"

Debbie nodded. "Well, you'll get an easy A then! We're just starting Japan." He gave her a copy of the class timetable and pointed out when gym class was. "You aren't in band, I don't think."

"Debbie plays basketball," Paige told him. "I've seen her play and she's pretty good. Mr. Anderson coaches the basketball team," she said to Debbie.

"Really? When are try-outs? You haven't chosen the team yet, have you?"

Mr. Anderson smiled. "No, not at all. Try-outs are this Thursday after school. Just wear your gym clothes."

The bell rang and the class filled with kids. Debbie stayed at her desk near Paige. It seemed to her that all the girls looked at her suspiciously. Had someone told them about her? Did they know she was adopted, that she used to get in trouble a lot at her old school? She tried to smile, like Greg had told her to. She tried to say hi when someone said hello to her but in the end she didn't think it made much difference. No one was going to like her in this new school, except Paige.

At the end of the day she walked home with Paige and then let herself into the quiet house. It felt kind of strange not having Nadine and Jason trailing along behind her, quarreling and whining. Poker greeted her with his usual enthusiasm and Angie smiled at her from the music room as Debbie passed.

"So, how did it go?" she asked.

"I don't think they liked me much." Debbie kicked off her shoes and hung her jacket in the closet.

"Wow, one whole day and the entire class doesn't like you? You must be pretty awful."

Debbie glared at Angie, swinging her backpack. "You said it, not me."

"Oh Deb, think about what you just said. How could the whole class make a decision about you that fast? You have to give people a chance to get to know you. Paige likes you. Jenna likes you."

That was true. "Well, maybe they don't all hate me. Just half," she said, but she was smiling.

8

Try-outs

It would have to snow today, of all days," Paige grumbled as she and Debbie walked to school. It had snowed all night and flakes were still falling as the girls crossed the street and made their way onto the school grounds.

"What difference does it make to you if it snows today or another day?" Debbie asked. She wasn't too thrilled that it had snowed either. Basketball try-outs were after school that day and she had been hoping to get in some practice before that. That was out of the question now, however.

"Because it's tonight that Mom and I go to Vancouver for that concert at the Orpheum. Remember? Mom hates driving in the snow. Especially all the way to Vancouver. She'll never agree to go now."

"I wouldn't worry about it now," Debbie told her, "wait until after school. They'll clear the roads by then."

But Paige wouldn't be comforted. "No, she already warned me that we probably wouldn't be able to go. And Scott was supposed to go to a basketball game, too. But that probably won't happen. Mom won't let him drive in with his friends if there is snow on the ground."

The two girls stood outside their classroom, watching the little kids play in the field while they waited for the bell. Debbie glanced down at her backpack, wondering if she had remembered to bring her gym clothes back to school. Mr. Anderson had warned the whole class that every day without shorts and a t-shirt would be a mark off. Plus, she wouldn't be able to do basketball try-outs without the right clothes.

She was very nervous about those try-outs. Greg had told her that she had nothing to worry about. If she tried her best and worked hard, then she would likely make the team. The trouble was, Debbie had never seen any of these kids play. She knew the kids at her old school. There was no way she and Jenna wouldn't have made that team. But this group was different. Lots of the girls were taller than Debbie, and there were a couple who were pretty aggressive in gym. She would die if she didn't make the team.

"Hey, there's Claudine. Claudine! Did you finish that worksheet on fractions?" Paige yelled.

A tall girl with long, dark hair and shiny black eyes approached them. Paige had told Debbie that Claudine was a pretty good basketball player and Debbie had been watching her carefully. How good was she? Her height was a bonus, that was for sure.

Claudine and Paige had been friends a long time. Ever since Claudine and her family had moved to Maple Ridge from Taiwan when Claudine was three. Eight years in one neighbourhood! It sounded like an eternity to Debbie who had never lived anywhere longer than four.

"Hey, Debbie. How's it going?" the girl asked, dropping her bag to the ground. She leaned against the wall. "Can you believe it snowed? My brother is skipping school today to go boarding. I wish I could."

"I'd never have the nerve," Paige said.

"Oh, it's no big deal. At the high school they don't check like they do here," Claudine told them. "He does it all the time. Hey, Debbie, are you trying out today for the team?"

"Yeah. Are you?"

"I think so. Practices are twice a week after school and I already have gymnastics and stuff, but it's only for a couple of months. Last year our team was one of the best. You any good?"

"Debbie is a great player. Her dad is a coach at the high school. He coaches Scott."

"Yeah? He been giving you pointers?"

"Some."

The bell rang and Mr. Anderson opened the door. Debbie put her stuff away and went to her desk. She was getting used to this new school, her new teacher and the kids. They were all right. Mr. Anderson was big on math and science, which was a pain. But Debbie was good at getting by with little effort and so far at home the most Angie and Greg had done was ask if she had finished all her homework and if she needed any help.

"Have you got that page of questions ready to hand in, Deb?" Mr. Anderson asked, stopping at her desk. He already had a pile of papers in his hand.

"Was that due today?" Debbie asked, frowning. "I thought it was next week. I'll hand it in tomorrow."

"Debbie, you knew it was due today. I reminded everyone yesterday. Stay in at lunch and finish it, please."

* * *

It seemed like the day would never end. Every time Debbie glanced at the clock it didn't seem to have moved at all. She got more and more nervous and uptight as the day went on. But finally, finally the bell rang at two thirty and she could grab her gym strip — that is, her shorts and t-shirt — and head to the change rooms.

The noise in the gym was deafening. Twenty girls had basketballs and were practicing their lay-ups and dribbling around the gym. Debbie grabbed a ball and found a corner to warm up in. Paige wasn't interested in basketball and couldn't play at all, but she sat on the stage to watch, giving Debbie a thumbs up any time she glanced over. It was kind of nice, her watching like that, giving Debbie some moral support. Debbie grinned at her. After about ten minutes, Mr. Anderson and Mrs. Williams, the coaches, called them over to the centre.

"We'll start with some warm-up drills then move on to some other drills before we play a mini game," Mr. Anderson told the girls. "Today I am looking at how you handle the ball, how you play with the other girls and how you listen to instructions. I don't want to have to repeat myself, so pay attention. If you don't understand something, then ask. Mrs. Williams and I might make some notes. Don't get freaked out if you see us writing while we look at you! Just have fun and try your best."

Mrs. Williams took over then, having them spread out around the gym. They spent the next ten minutes stretching, jumping, running, all the boring stuff that Debbie hated. She just wanted to get on with it.

"Isn't this a drag? I hate this part," a girl Debbie didn't know whispered as they each got a ball from the bin.

"Yeah. I just want to get on to a game."

"Really. But Mrs. Williams and Mr. Anderson are big on 'fundamentals' and all that. You're new here, aren't you? You play before?"

"Yeah, at my old school."

"I'm Sarah. Sarah Percy."

"Debbie ... Lowell," Debbie told her, blushing as she always did when using her new last name.

"I'm in Mr. McGregor's class. You in Mr. Anderson's?"

Before Debbie could answer, Mrs. Williams had called for their attention. She divided the group into two and Mr. Anderson took half and she took the other half. Sarah and Debbie found themselves still together.

"So where do you live?" Sarah asked as they worked on their dribbling.

"Across the street, brown house."

"Oh yeah. I live around the corner at the McLeod's place. Big old house with a stupid purple door."

Debbie grinned. "Why'd your parents put in a purple door?" she asked. It seemed like a strange colour for a door.

"They aren't my parents," Sarah said shortly and moved away.

Debbie watched her go, thinking. Of course, Sarah had said her name was Percy, not McLeod. Debbie was willing to bet Sarah was a foster kid. Debbie felt a small surge of sympathy. She knew how Sarah felt! Debbie had never wanted to tell anyone she was in foster care either. It was embarrassing.

They practiced drills for nearly forty-five minutes before dividing into small groups for some three-on-three. Debbie was put in as a point guard to begin, which was her favourite position, with Claudine and another girl named Erika, against Sarah, and two other girls Debbie hadn't met.

The ball was tipped to Debbie off the jump ball. She dribbled a bit and then passed to Claudine. Claudine drove for the basket, stopped at the top of the key, looked up to see Sarah in her way and bounced the ball back to Debbie. Debbie broke hard for the basket, went up and laid it in.

One of Sarah's teammates picked up the ball and dribbled toward centre, then lost control when Claudine challenged her and the ball rolled into the other game. It was tricky playing on half a court. There wasn't as much room, although there weren't as many players either. It was kind of like playing outside at lunch. Claudine caught the in-bound pass and broke fast, until she was held up when Sarah got in front of her. Claudine spun on her pivot foot, then back again, trying to lose Sarah, then finally passed to Erika. Erika caught the pass, side-stepped the girl from the other team, drove for the basket and made the two points.

The other team took the rebound and moved up court. The girl tried to pass, but Debbie intercepted and dribbled all the way back down court. Sarah appeared in front of her, out of nowhere, but Debbie drove for the basket and made a beautiful fade-away jump shot right over Sarah's head.

"Yes!" she said to herself as she landed then turned and caught Mr. Anderson's thumbs up. She flushed, but grinned happily.

They played for ten minutes and then Debbie's group sat down while another six had a turn. Debbie wiped at her forehead as she leaned against the wall. It felt so good to play! If she didn't make the team, she didn't know what she'd do. Watching some of the others, she knew she had some tough competition. Still, going over the try-out in her mind, she didn't think she'd done too badly.

"Okay, girls, that's it for today. The roster will be posted outside the gym doors by next Friday. Yes, I know," Mr. Anderson said as a groan went up, "but you have to give us time to think about it. You all looked good today. Good job."

Debbie changed quickly and met Paige at the doors. She was starving and Poker would be getting impatient for his walk.

"I thought you looked great, Debbie," Paige said.

"Thanks. We don't find out until next Friday. That's forever."

"I know you'll make it!"

"Thanks. And Paige," Debbie continued, "thanks for staying to watch today. It was nice of you."

Paige grinned and shook her head, her red hair flapping against her cheeks. "We're friends, aren't we?" she asked and Debbie nodded. Somehow in the weeks she had been visiting Angie and Greg, she and Paige had become friends.

"Well," Paige said, "that's what friends do, right? Moral support or whatever? See ya tomorrow!"

9

Making the Team

The next day Claudine joined Paige and Debbie as they headed outside at recess. She offered them each a cookie as they walked along the path. "I don't know how I'm going to make it through next week," she said. "Why can't they make up their minds faster than that?"

Debbie shrugged. "I guess they're busy with other stuff."

"She's not really that calm," Paige told Claudine with a giggle. "You should have heard her this morning."

They made their way to the back of the playground, out of the way of the little kids and their snow forts. Debbie noticed Sarah Percy a short way off talking with some girls. She wanted to say something to the other girl, something about being a foster kid, but before she could say anything, Claudine had pulled her attention away.

"So did you play basketball at your old school, Debbie?" she asked.

"Yeah. Well, I never played on the team, you had to be in grade six. But we played a lot outside."

"So how come your parents moved here?"

"They didn't!" Paige said before Debbie could answer.

"Paige," Debbie started, grabbing Paige's arm.

"Well tell her!"

"Tell me what?" Claudine asked, glancing from one girl to the other.

"Debbie was adopted! By the Lowells! Over Christmas!" Paige's clear voice rang out over the snow till Debbie was certain everyone on the playground had heard her. She blushed and shuffled her feet uncomfortably on the slippery path. Over Claudine's shoulder, she caught Sarah's surprised glance.

"Really? That's cool. I thought only babies were adopted. Do you like them?" Claudine asked.

Debbie scooped up a handful of snow and formed it into a smooth, round ball, then threw it at a tree. It missed and landed with a splat on the ground. "They're nice, I guess."

"So why were you adopted? What happened to your mom and dad?"

Debbie could see that Sarah was still listening. Maybe hearing Debbie's story would give the other girl hope. Debbie had never thought she would be adopted, and look what had happened. She cleared her throat.

"Well, my birth mom couldn't take care of me so I went to live with a foster family when I was four. Then they moved away and I went to the Barkers and lived with them for about three years."

"Did you get to choose your new mom and dad?" Claudine wondered.

"Well, they kind of chose me," Debbie explained, "but I could have said no."

"I wish I could pick my parents. Mine are such a drag," Claudine said and Paige grinned, nodding her head in agreement.

Just then Sarah passed them with her friends. She caught Debbie's eye and scowled at her, her face hard and unfriendly.

"What's her problem?" Claudine asked.

"I don't know," Debbie told her, stunned at Sarah's nasty look.

"Maybe it's because you're better than her at basketball," Paige suggested.

"Don't worry about her, Deb," Claudine told her. "Sarah has a problem with lots of people. She doesn't like me because my family is from Taiwan." She shrugged.

"Yeah, and she doesn't like Nicole because Nicole is from Hong Kong. She doesn't like me much because I'm red-headed."

Debbie nodded, feeling better. It sounded like it was more Sarah's problem than Debbie's. She didn't have any more chance to worry about it, however, because Claudine had changed the subject.

"Hey, see that tree there? I bet I can nail it with this snowball," Claudine told them, forming a snowball.

"From way back here?"

"Sure. I play softball in the spring. I have a pretty good arm." She wound up and threw, and sure enough, the snowball hit the tree trunk.

"We could get in trouble if a teacher sees us," Paige warned them. "We're not supposed to throw snowballs on school property."

Claudine stuck out her tongue and scooped another handful of snow from the ground. "So keep an eye out for teachers, then. Besides, we're not throwing them at anyone. Your turn," she said, handing Debbie a snowball. She threw it quickly, poorly. The snow hit the ground at the base of the tree.

"Try again!" Claudine told her, handing her another. "And aim better this time. Haven't you ever played baseball or softball?"

Debbie shook her head. The only thing she was any good at was basketball. This time she aimed for a tree closer to her and hit it.

"Let me try," Paige demanded. She smoothed her snowball, threw, then laughed hysterically as it landed a good three feet away from the tree.

The three girls continued trying to hit the tree with their snowballs until the bell rang. In the end Debbie was actually hitting more than she missed. At the bell they walked slowly back toward the school, discussing who might make the team.

* * *

Friday arrived eventually. At lunch Debbie ate quickly then got herself outside. It was clear and cold and the sunlight sparkled off the snow. There were snow forts and the remains of snow people all over the field, but there were lots of bare patches too.

Debbie carefully molded a big snowball, looking around her quickly before she threw it at a tree. She didn't need any more warnings from inflexible teachers caught up in their silly rules. She hit the tree perfectly and smiled to herself. She was getting better with all the practice she'd had all week. Maybe she would ask Greg about trying out for baseball in the spring.

"Nice arm," Claudine said, arriving with Paige.

Debbie grinned self-consciously. "Thanks," she muttered, bending over to pick up more snow.

"They post the list today."

"I know." Debbie smoothed her snowball with her glove then wound up, throwing as she turned. "Ooops!" she cried, covering her mouth with her hand as the snowball shattered against the back of a boy's head.

"Oh, Debbie," Paige whispered. "You're going to catch it this time."

The boy turned around and saw the three girls standing behind him. Claudine and Paige were trying hard not to laugh. Debbie looked stricken. He gaped at her, his eyes growing wet with tears. In another second he had bolted across the field toward a supervisor.

"Let's go back to class," Claudine suggested and the three girls ran for the school.

Debbie thought that lousy afternoon would last forever. She was given a whole week of lunchtime detentions as well as having to write an apology to the boy. Plus, she had left some work at home and Mr. Anderson's frown and head-shaking told her he was losing patience. She didn't care, she just wanted the day to be over so she could check the team list.

When the bell rang at last Debbie bolted from the room with Claudine and Paige. They pushed through the crowd of girls standing around the list outside the gym.

Her stomach did flips and her mouth was dry as she read down the row of names. But there she was, Debbie Lowell. A grin spread across her face. She couldn't wait to go home and tell Greg.

* * *

They had a celebratory dinner that night in honour of Debbie making the basketball team, and then Angie and Debbie went to the high school to watch Greg's team play an exhibition game. Debbie had never been to a basketball game as a spectator before. It was so exciting sitting in the stands with the other fans cheering good plays and booing when the opposition had possession of the ball.

Debbie loved the squeak of the rubber-soled sneakers on the well-polished floor and the thud-thud-thud of the ball as it was dribbled from end to end and the calls of the players as they passed to each other. She liked looking at the Sentinels' bench, at the row of boys, in their turquoise and white jerseys and shorts, and at Greg, standing behind the players, wearing a suit and his basketball tie.

Greg's team was pretty good. The other team, the Marauders, weren't as tall or as quick. Debbie very quickly got the hang of reading the names on the backs of the jerseys to keep track of who was who.

The Sentinels' centre, a boy named Morrison, took the tip-off and passed the ball to a guy named Webber. Webber bolted toward the basket, laying it up for a quick two points. The crowd cheered, calling, "Web-bie, Web-bie!" The Marauders took the rebound and play quickly passed to the other end of the court.

"Defense! Defense!" the crowd cried. Collins, the Sentinel defender, stuck with his player like glue, and seemed to be doing a good job of containing him. The guy spun this way and that, pivoting on first one foot then the other, trying to get away from him. In the end he managed to dish the ball off to another player, but not before Collins collided with him.

"Personal foul, number twenty-seven, Sentinels," the ref announced to the score-keeper and the crowd booed.

The Marauder player took the ball from the ref and stood on the foul line, bouncing the ball once, twice, a third time. Then he spun it in his hands, his eyes on the net. Debbie clenched her fists between her knees. Around her the crowd pounded their feet on the metal floor of the bleachers. The noise was deafening but the player didn't seem concerned. He lined up his shot, aimed and tossed it up. It came down in a graceful arch and went through the rings without even touching the sides. The crowd booed again. He missed the second shot and a cheer went up. Debbie grabbed Angie's arm and shook her in excitement, then let go, embarrassed. "Sorry," she muttered, her face red.

"That's okay, Deb," Angie said. "I might do the same to you!"

In the next second, the whistle blew again and the ref pointed at another Sentinel player. Greg's voice rose above the noise of the crowd. He shook his fist and his face went red. Debbie smiled at Greg's antics.

"He gets pretty riled up, doesn't he?" Angie asked, catching sight of her smile.

"I'll say. But he was right, that was a bad call."

"This ref is new to the job, I think. I don't recognize him," Angie told her.

"Yeah? Do you come to lots of the games?" Debbie asked, surprised. It had never occured to her that Angie would like basketball.

"Most of them. I like basketball. Greg and I used to go to the Grizzlies games when they played in Vancouver. We had seasons tickets."

"It's so lousy that they're gone," Debbie said. She had never gone to a game, but she had watched them on television when Steve would let her. "I liked their uniforms."

"Me too. And I really liked Mike Bibby," Angie whispered, grinning.

"My favourite was Sharif, though," Debbie told her.

"Yeah, he was a pretty amazing player."

Debbie caught Angie's eye and they smiled at each other before Debbie looked back at the floor. She wondered why Angie had never said anything about liking basketball before. But then, Debbie reminded herself, Debbie had never asked either. She had just assumed Angie was not the sporty type. She smiled again. She was kind of glad she had been wrong.

In the end Greg's team won, sixty-eight to sixty-two. His team crowded around him and the other coaches, patting each other on the back and shoulders, giving each other high fives. A few of the players, including Pete Webber, rubbed Greg on the top of the head.

Angie and Debbie went down to the floor once the crowd had thinned and congratulated Greg and the boys on their win. Greg kissed Angie and put his arm around Debbie's shoulder. He grinned at her.

"Hey guys, I'd like you to meet my daughter, Deb. Deb, these are the guys."

A chorus of hellos went up but gradually the guys disappeared to the locker room to shower and change.

"Well, what did you think?" Greg asked, gathering some forgotten towels. "How'd my boys do?"

"It was cool. They sure are fast. And tall! I wish I could just sink a basket the way that Pete Webber did. He was awesome."

"Yes, Pete is a great player. We're going to miss him when he graduates in June. Some university is going to snap him up. But hopefully he'll remember his old high school coach and speak of me fondly."

"For heaven's sake, Greg," Angie said, shaking her head. Still, she was laughing.

10

Old Habits

The team's very first practice was the following Tuesday after school. Debbie met up with Claudine in the changing room and they quickly got into their gym strip and hightops. Debbie pulled a scrunchie out of her bag and tied her hair back from her face.

"You ready for this?" Claudine asked. "I've heard that Mrs. Williams is pretty tough."

"Oh, I can handle it," Debbie said. "Greg's been giving me lots of pointers and stuff." A couple of girls on the bench opposite Debbie, Sarah included, glanced over, eyebrows raised.

"Maybe he can give me some tips, too," Claudine said. She shoved her clothes in her gym bag and stood up.

"Well, he is the high school coach, so he knows what he's talking about. Paige's brother, Scott, says he's a good coach, and he should know, he's had lots of them."

Claudine was right, though. Mrs. Williams and Mr. Anderson ran a tough practice. They ran through the same warm-up they'd had for try-outs, and then very quickly they were divided into two groups to work on drills. Debbie felt pretty confident during the drills. They were mostly easy things that she had been taught before or had worked on with Greg. She kept an eye on the others, though, wondering about the other girls. Sarah was pretty good, and Claudine was doing better than she had during try-outs. Two of the girls she'd played against in the mini-game were fast, but a lot of the others were still learning. She hoped they didn't slow the good players down too much.

Part way through the practice Mr. Anderson called Debbie up to the front to help him demonstrate another exercise. Debbie grinned as she ran up and stood beside him, facing the other girls. She put her shoulders back and looked around, proud of herself. A lot of the girls frowned and looked away. What was their problem? Debbie wondered. Jealous, she guessed, because she had Greg giving her extra help, making her better than they were.

Debbie ignored them as she paired up with Claudine to work the new drill. She took up her position as defensive rebounder while Claudine took up the block position just behind her. Mr. Anderson threw the ball at the net from the foul line.

"Shot!" Debbie cried, pushing backwards into Claudine as she jumped to catch the ball.

"Good, Deb. Make sure you keep low, though, you were a bit high in your stance. Okay, switch girls."

They switched positions and then headed for the end of the line. Sarah and her partner glanced at Claudine and Debbie but then looked quickly away.

"It must be nice to have a dad who's a coach," Sarah said to her friend.

"Yeah. I don't know if I would bother hanging out with a bunch of beginners," the friend answered.

"I think I'd probably just go try out for the high school team."

"If you have something to say," Claudine said, poking the taller girl on the shoulder, "you should just say it." But the two girls just scowled and turned away, saying nothing.

* * *

It didn't take long for the snow to melt from the playground and by the fourth week of January it was dry enough that the basketball court could be used. Debbie bolted out the door at lunch as soon as she finished eating, basketball in hand, ready for a good game. She wanted to work on some of the techniques they were learning in practice. Their first game, against Mount Goldie, was on Monday, and she wanted to be great.

She was the first one on the court, so she worked by herself on her foul shots. Greg had suggested that she try closing her eyes and visualizing the ball leaving her fingers and traveling through the air and through the net before actually shooting. In the mini-games during practice it had worked pretty well.

"Hey, it's the little kids' turn to use the court," a voice said. Debbie opened her eyes to find a boy standing holding a basketball. He looked like he was about nine. Debbie ignored him.

"You're not supposed to be on the court today," he said again. "It's our turn. You can play on the playground."

Debbie laughed. "Yeah, like I want to go down the slide," she said. "You can't even reach the basket, why do you want to play? You go play on the slide."

"We have to take turns."

Debbie turned away and threw another foul shot. This one hit the rim and bounced off. She ran to get it.

"I'm telling!" the boy said, finally realizing that Debbie was not going to leave.

"What a tattletale," she called after him. "Can't you fight your own battles?"

He came back with a supervisor, an older woman with gray hair and a bright green coat. "Primary day on the courts, today," she told Debbie. "Intermediate tomorrow."

"There was no one out here. If they aren't going to use it, the big kids should be allowed to. And besides, did you notice there aren't any big kids on the playground?"

"The rule is there to keep things fair. It doesn't matter if only two kids want to play basketball, it is their day. You'll have to wait until tomorrow."

"That is the stupidest rule I ever heard. Who comes up with them? 'Cause they don't make much sense."

"If you'd like, you can take it up with Mr. Vanelli. I'm sure he'd love to hear your thoughts on his rules. In the meantime, off the court."

"He can't even reach the net with the ball! I could stay and give him some pointers," Debbie tried. The supervisor took a step toward her and Debbie backed away. "Man, this school sucks," she said, glaring at the supervisor as she walked off the court. She spent the rest of the noon hour leaning against the wall of the school, bouncing her ball as low to the ground as she could, glaring at the little kid on the court with his short legs. He never once got it in the net, she noticed. Stupid rule.

After lunch the first three assignments for the unit on Japan were due. Debbie sat slumped in her desk, arms folded across her chest. She had finished the one on culture, there were some pictures Greg had helped her find on the internet and from some magazines and the bibliography. But the other two parts, recreation and food, she hadn't even started. She had told Angie, when she had asked, that they weren't due at the same time.

Beside her Paige was putting the finishing touches on her assignment. She had beautifully drawn illustrations, nicely coloured and labeled, a table of contents and a bibliography all bound together in a report cover. Watching her reminded Debbie of Jenna. Jenna had always had her work done on time, neat and complete. Debbie squirmed in her seat. Would Mr. Anderson tell Angie and Greg? What would they do?

There was other work that hadn't been completed or handed in, too. Stuff the teacher had been asking for.

Mr. Anderson asked them to hand in their assignments, and Paige offered to take Debbie's up when she took her own. For the moment, anyway, she was safe from the lecture she knew would come. Teachers were such a drag about work.

At the end of the day Debbie shoved her books and lunch bag into her pack and then waited to walk with Paige. They made their way out of the school, down the road the short distance to Paige's house.

"You want to come in?"

Debbie glanced across to her own house. There was no extra car in the driveway at that second, but there would be soon. Little Tiffany Myers came on Wednesdays with her cloth bag of beginners' notebooks. Debbie hated Tiffany's lesson, it would be nice not to have to hear it. Debbie grinned at Paige. "I'll call Angie and tell her I'm here," she said.

"I'll show you that new book on 5th Avenue I got from my Nana," Paige told her as they let themselves in the front door.

"You mean the band that's all brothers or something?"

"Yeah! Haven't you heard them? I have all their CDs. They are so cool, Deb. Come on I'll play it for you." Paige grabbed Debbie's hand and hauled her up the stairs to her room.

Debbie had been in Paige's room often since that first Saturday. It was green and yellow and reminded Debbie of vegetables, but the best thing about it was the TV. Paige had her own television. It only got two channels, and they were fuzzy most of the time, but a TV was a TV. Debbie wondered if Greg would get her one if she asked.

They listened to the CD and looked through the pages of the book, then Paige made them ice-cream sundaes which they ate in front of the colour television that got all the channels.

Around four-thirty Debbie figured she'd better go home. She thanked Paige for the ice cream and said good-bye to

Scott, who barely noticed her leaving, then let herself out the front door.

Angie was sitting at the piano in the music room talking on the phone when Debbie came in. Debbie kicked off her shoes then got down on her knees to greet Poker, who washed her face with happy kisses. "I'm going to take you out for a walk," she murmured to him, stroking his ears.

Angie hung up the phone and turned slightly on the stool so she could see Debbie. "I'm glad you're home," she said, laying the phone on the piano.

"I was just going to walk Poker."

"Good. But first I want to talk to you. That was Mr. Anderson."

Here it was, then, Debbie realized. The call from school. She sat perfectly still and said nothing.

"Let's go sit in the family room," Angie said. Debbie followed her slowly into the other room and sat on the couch beside her.

"He told me you haven't been handing things in on time. Some of the things he told me were late you told me weren't even due. He said you haven't been finishing your math, and there are a couple of reading assignments he hasn't seen yet that were due several days ago. Don't you want to do well in your new school?" Angie asked.

Debbie examined the dirt under her fingernail, wondering where it had come from. Was it chocolate sauce from the sundae? She stuck her finger in her mouth and tried to get it out. Angie pulled her hand away.

"Please don't do that," Angie said. "Would you answer my question?"

"I don't care how I do at school!" Debbie said, jumping up from the couch. "Half the stuff is stupid and doesn't make any sense."

"If the work is too much for you, you need to tell us so we can help, or Mr. Anderson can help. Not doing your homework and lying about it is not the answer."

"I don't care about any of it! What difference does it make if I can add fractions? It's all stupid!"

Greg came in then, catching her last words. He put his briefcase down and joined them in the family room. Angie was still sitting on the couch but Debbie had moved to the corner by the door. She glared at Angie and stuck her finger back in her mouth. She tuned out as Angie explained what had happened to Greg.

"You lied to us?" Greg asked when she had finished. Debbie felt guilty twinges creep up and down her spine and refused to look at him. "Answer me, please."

She shrugged. "I guess. Sort of."

"Mr. Anderson and I have decided that from now on you will show him your planner before you leave at the end of the day," Angie said. "He will make sure you have what you need to complete the work and that you have written everything down. Then, each night, your father or I will go over everything with you and make sure it's done. We will help you get it finished if you're having trouble."

"No way! That's not fair!" Debbie cried.

"We had hoped that you would take some responsibility for yourself, Deb," Greg told her softly. "We didn't want to start our new life together by checking up on you and making a lot of rules, but you aren't trying."

"This sucks. You suck. Both of you! I wish I had never moved here!" She bolted from the room and up the stairs and finally slammed the door to her room, throwing herself across the bed. Having parents stank. It was worse that being a foster kid. At least foster parents left her alone!

11

First Game

Despite Debbie's feelings on the subject, every afternoon Mr. Anderson held out his hand for her planner. He looked through her pile of books to make sure she had what she needed and then he initialed the page so her parents knew it had been seen. He tried to make it as inconspicuous as he could, but Debbie still felt like all eyes were on her, that they were all laughing at her. It was no better at home. She had to sit down to her homework as soon as she had walked Poker and after dinner either Greg or Angie looked it over to make sure it was done.

She looked longingly at her suitcases, packed and ready in the closet, but she couldn't walk back to Delta — she didn't even know if the Barkers would take her — and where else was there to go? A couple of times she considered calling Leanne but something stopped her. She had a funny feeling Leanne would be on Greg's and Angie's side on this.

Thursday afternoon Debbie got held up with Mr. Anderson and was late getting to the changing room before practice. Nicole was just tucking things in her bag when Debbie came in but everyone else had left. Debbie sat on the bench and began changing.

"Isn't this the cutest thing you ever saw?" Nicole asked. "My dad brought it back from Hong Kong for me. It's from my grandma."

Debbie glanced over at the little plush zebra. Jenna had lots of those stuffed animals; they were lined up on her bookshelf, but Debbie didn't get the attraction. She'd rather have a real pet, like Poker. "He's pretty cute," she agreed. "I've never seen that one before."

"I have lots of them, but I think he's my favourite." Nicole tucked the zebra into her gym bag and the two girls left the room together.

Practice was hard that day, to get ready for the game the following Monday. The coaches worked them nonstop for the full hour, with lots of three-on-threes and drills. They talked about strategies and game plans. One of the plays they worked on for a long time was the pick-and-roll.

First Mr. Anderson had Claudine stand at the top of the key, pretending to defend while Nicole took a jump shot. When Claudine broke for the basket, Nicole tossed a pass to her as she ran and Claudine jumped up and laid it in. After a while they switched and Debbie and Sarah took over. Debbie was the plant, Sarah the passer. The first time they tried it, Sarah's pass went wide and Debbie couldn't catch it.

"That's okay," she called, "try again." Sarah glared at her.

"I don't need you coaching me," she said under her breath as they passed each other.

"I was just being encouraging," Debbie said, hurt.

"Well don't bother."

They got back in position and tried again. This time Debbie caught the pass and laid it up and in. They ran it over and over until the two girls were perfect, then another two tried.

Finally, Mrs. Williams ended practice and the girls dragged themselves into the changing room. Debbie sank onto the bench by her things and pulled off her shoes. Nicole came in and opened her bag to pull out her clothes. Debbie glanced up as she finished tying her shoes and saw Nicole frantically pawing through her bag.

"Did any of you see my stuffed zebra?" she asked. "It was just here, poking out of my bag."

A chorus of no's went up around the room. A few girls helped her look, picking up shirts and socks lying on the bench, looking under the bench, but the zebra was gone.

Nicole sat down on the bench, her empty bag in her hands. She looked close to tears. "What could have happened to it?" she asked, her voice catching. She looked up and caught Debbie's eye. "You know what it looks like," she said. "Did you see anything suspicious?"

"No. Sorry," Debbie told her.

"Someone must have taken it," Nicole said.

"But who would do that? Who knew it was here besides you and Deb?" Claudine asked.

Debbie grabbed her bag off the hook and headed for the door. It was too bad about Nicole's zebra, she thought. Someone must have come in during practice and seen it. As she swung the door open, she turned her head and found Sarah staring at her. The other girl narrowed her eyes, her mouth tight. Debbie flushed and turned away, hurrying through the door. What was her problem? she wondered.

At home she dumped her bag on a chair in the kitchen and rummaged through the fridge for something to eat. There was a note on the counter from Angie, who was teaching.

"Dear Debbie; Could you start dinner once you've taken Poker out? I owe you one! And also, Jenna called. She can stay over next weekend. Give her a call later to decide a time. Also, please empty the dishwasher. Love Mom."

Debbie thought her jaw would crack from the grin she wore. Finally! Finally Jenna was coming. She grabbed the phone, forgetting all about Poker, waiting for his walk, the dishwasher waiting to be emptied and the dinner waiting to be started. How would she ever make it through ten days? she wondered.

* * *

No one said anything else about the incident in the changing room, although Nicole's stuffed zebra never re-appeared, and after a few days, no one but Nicole even remembered that the toy had been taken in the first place.

Their first game, against the Wildcats, was an away game. The Silverdene Stars wore their green and white away jerseys. It was strange to be in an unfamiliar gym with strange girls and spectators who weren't cheering for them when they scored a basket. But tucked in a corner were Angie and Greg, who had canceled his own team's practice that afternoon just to be there. Debbie grinned at them and waved.

Mr. Anderson started the game with Debbie at centre. The Wildcat's centre was a little taller than Debbie and her fingers just managed to reach the ball, sending it into the hands of a waiting forward. The Wildcat forward charged up court and tried to sink a long shot, but missed. Claudine picked up the rebound and dribbled back toward centre. Just past the mid-court line a Wildcat reached in to grab the ball away from her. The Wildcat rushed through the middle. The jump shot went in seamlessly and a roar went up from the crowd.

Debbie took the throw-in and stood for a second, watching the floor as she dribbled. There were Wildcats everywhere she looked, it seemed. Their outstretched arms were like a forest of tall, gangly trees blocking her view. How she wanted to do well while Greg was watching her! She bolted to the left, then stopped abruptly and went right, narrowly missing the Wildcats' tall centre.

"Pass!" Sarah screamed from somewhere to her left. Debbie looked up, found Sarah and passed her the ball then broke for the basket. Sarah passed back to Debbie who banged it home and the Stars had tied the game. She glanced at Greg, who was standing, clapping loudly. He gave her a thumbs up and she grinned.

Play went back and forth pretty evenly. Although the Stars were quicker on their feet and better at sinking the foul shots, the Wildcats were taller and better at sinking their outside jump shots. By halftime the two teams were tied at twenty.

The second half started and the Stars came out hard. Debbie was the player to beat and the other Stars kept feeding her the ball. She seldom missed but when she did either Claudine or Sarah managed to get the rebound. Unfortunately, their defense wasn't that great and so they kept trading baskets with their opponents. The Wildcats were excellent passers, using all sorts of different give-and-goes to get the ball around the court. The Stars' defense began to break down. One player, a tall, dark-haired girl wearing number thirty, seemed to be everywhere, dodging and feinting, moving this way and that across the key. She was constantly getting away from her defender, just when one of her teammates was set to feed her the ball, and scoring.

Finally Mrs. Williams called a time out and gathered the Stars around her at the bench. She made a couple of substitutions and then explained what she wanted them to do. When the ref blew the whistle to start play again she looked around, waiting for a nod of understanding from each player. Everyone knew what their job was.

Back on the court, Debbie set herself up between number thirty and the basket. That was her job. No matter where the girl was, Debbie was to be between her and the Wildcat's basket. The other Stars players fanned out across the court. Every time a Wildcat player tried to pass to number thirty, there was a Star waiting to intercept. As pass after pass was picked off, the Stars gradually moved out in front. It was working!

In the end the Stars won forty-two to thirty-seven. Debbie came out of the dressing room to find Greg and Angie waiting for her.

"I can't believe we won!" she cried, hugging him. "That was so amazing. Did you see when that Wildcat tried to throw me off? I thought I'd never lose her!"

"We're very proud of you." Angie said, smiling. "You played hard the whole time you were on the floor and your whole team looked good together."

"We're just going to wait for Claudine, okay? She needs a ride home."

The others passed on their way out of the gym. Nicole gave Debbie a high five and a couple of the others waved and called "Good game." Then Sarah emerged from the changing room. She saw Debbie standing with Greg and Angie, scowled and looked quickly away. Debbie blushed and scuffed her shoe against the floor.

"Who was that, Deb?" Angie asked softly.

"Oh, her name is Sarah."

"She didn't seem very pleased about something."

Debbie looked up at her. "She says I think I'm better than everyone else because Greg's a coach." She shrugged. "She has a bad attitude. And she doesn't like anyone anyway, Paige says."

"Do you think you're better than everyone else because I'm a coach?" Greg asked.

"No. I'm just good at basketball, that's all. I think she's jealous. I can't help it that you're a coach or that the coaches pick me to help with drills."

"You are a good player, Deb," Greg told her, "but so are lots of these other girls. It's important to play as a team and support one another. Other players won't like it if you start throwing it up in their faces that your dad is a coach."

"I don't!"

"Okay! Good! Here's Claudine. Shall we get home? I'm hungry."

12

Accusations

"And this is my room," Debbie said proudly, pushing the door open. It had been cleaned very carefully that morning before Debbie and Greg had gone to New Westminster to pick up Jenna. The bed was neatly made, the clothes were hung up or folded away in the dresser, there were no plates or glasses lying around and all the games and CDs and magazines were on the shelves.

Jenna looked around her, her eyes wide. She grinned when she spotted the photograph on the desk. "This is awesome, Deb," she said, going in. "You are so lucky. I wish my parents would let me have a CD player in my room. But no, Carlie and I have to share. It isn't fair — she always hogs it. And check out this poster! Where'd you get it?" she asked, staring up at the framed poster of Steve Nash hanging above the bed.

"Christmas. Greg got me the magazine he was in, too."

"And look at all the books! Have you read any of them?" Jenna asked, scanning the shelves. She pulled a couple of books off to have a better look, quickly reading the back covers. "This one is great," she said, holding up a book called *Great Lengths*. "I did a book report on it last year."

"I haven't read any of them. They were all Angie's. Some were Greg's."

"You should. These are good. Wow, this one is even signed! That is so cool!"

Debbie sat on the edge of the bed, watching as her friend moved around the room, oohing and aahing over Debbie's belongings. It felt good to have things, to have a room that Jenna wished she could have. She had never owned anything someone else wanted before. Mostly it felt so good just to have Jenna in the same room. She looked almost exactly like she had the last time Debbie had seen her. Her hair was longer and she had pink nail polish on her fingertips, but otherwise she was just Jenna. Here to stay for one whole night.

"So how's your new school? Any cool girls? Who's that Paige you were telling me about?" Jenna asked, finally coming to sit beside Debbie on the bed.

"Oh, Paige lives across the street. You'll probably meet her — she's been asking about you. But she's pretty nice. Her brother, Scott, plays on Greg's team at the high school."

"Oh yeah. Is the team at your new school any good? We have a pretty good team but we miss you at centre, let me tell you. That Nicki Ellison is such a pathetic crybaby. She's tall, but she doesn't know how to play."

"There's a couple of girls like that on the Stars. We won our first game, though. And Greg and Angie came to watch. He said I played really well," Debbie told her, still proud of the twelve points she had made that day.

"You told me! We won our first one too! Too bad we can't play each other. That would be so cool." There was a silence for a minute and then Jenna cleared her throat. "Say Deb, do you mind if I ask you a question?"

"Go ahead."

"Well, I just wondered, you know, why you still call Angie and Greg by their names and not Mom and Dad. You don't have to tell me, I just wondered. Maybe it isn't any of my business."

Debbie flushed and looked away from Jenna. Leanne had told her, in one of their many talks about the adoption and what would happen, that she could call her new parents whatever she felt most comfortable calling them. She had said that even though Greg and Angie would really like her to call them Mom and Dad, they understood if Debbie didn't at first. Debbie wondered, sometimes, when she would feel comfortable. So far it hadn't happened. It was still hard even thinking of them as her parents.

"I don't know," she said softly, playing with the comforter. "It's just hard, that's all. I try, sometimes, but the words won't come out." She shrugged.

"But it's okay here? I mean, you like it all right and everything?"

Debbie thought of the two suitcases in the closet and the homework police she had to go through every night. Then she thought of Poker and Greg and Angie cheering her when she'd scored at the game. "It's pretty good, I guess. I love my room and Angie is an amazing cook. Plus they aren't huge on rules, really. Except homework." She made a face and Jenna laughed.

"Someone is making you do your homework?" she asked, shoving playfully at Debbie's shoulder. "It's about time."

"Hey, you want to go outside with Poker and shoot some hoops? Or we could play on the computer. Greg has some wicked games."

* * *

Monday morning Debbie caught up to Paige at the end of her driveway and they walked the rest of the way together.

"Who was that girl I saw you with?" she demanded.

"That was my friend, Jenna, from Delta. Remember? I told you she was coming for a visit this weekend."

"Oh. Well, you could have introduced me."

"Sorry. Maybe next time, okay? I was kind of excited to see her. Did you have a good weekend? How was the recital?" Debbie asked.

"Pretty lame, actually," Paige told her. She giggled into her hand. "One of the fairies split her tights! It was a riot."

"I've never been to a dance recital before."

"Maybe I'll get Mom to buy you a ticket next time we go. We go all the time. It's pretty cool. I'll never dance like they do, though, that's for sure. Say, do you have practice today?"

"Yeah. Game Wednesday, practice Thursday. It's a busy week."

"Make sure you win, 'kay?" Paige told her. Debbie cuffed her, laughing.

* * *

As usual, practice was intense that afternoon. In one drill Debbie found herself paired up against Sarah. The other girl shot her a dirty look and tried to reposition herself, but the girl behind her shoved her back into her spot. Debbie took her position under the net, ignoring Sarah. Mrs. Williams tossed the ball against the backboard.

"Ball!" Debbie cried, catching it.

"Outlet!" Sarah called. Debbie passed her the ball then ran wide down the floor while Sarah dribbled the ball to the other foul line. Debbie caught the bounce pass and laid it up. Sarah caught the rebound, passed to Debbie and Debbie dribbled back to their starting point. She made a bounce pass to Sarah near the other net, but Sarah wasn't in position and missed it.

Debbie said nothing as the other girl ran after the ball. She took up her position again to wait for her next turn.

"She's not very good," Claudine whispered to her.

"She thinks she is, though," Nicole added. "And she doesn't like anyone telling her how to do something. Look at her scowling at Mr. Anderson! She's going to get kicked off the team if she acts like that."

"I heard her mouthing off the ref at the game last week," Claudine told them. "Mr. Anderson had to grab her pretty quick before she got thrown out of the game."

Debbie listened but said nothing. She didn't want to give Sarah any reason to dislike her anymore than she already did.

Practice ended at three-thirty and the girls grabbed their water bottles and headed for the change rooms. Everyone was chattering and laughing when suddenly there was a little cry of alarm.

"Has anyone seen my wallet?" Claudine asked, looking around the room. "It was in my backpack, in the pocket. There wasn't any money in it, but it was new."

"Not again!" Nicole cried.

"I'm going to get Mrs. Williams," Sarah said, throwing Debbie a dirty look as she left the room. Debbie finished tying her laces. Did Sarah think she had stolen the wallet? Why would she take her friend's things?

"What's going on in here, girls?" the teacher asked, coming back with Sarah a few minutes later. "Sarah said things have been going missing."

"First my zebra and now Claudine's wallet," Nicole told her.

"Girls, we're a team. You can't play as a team if you don't trust each other. I hope that whoever has taken the wallet and the zebra will return them, no questions asked, before school tomorrow. They can leave them on my desk. And from now on, you girls make sure you leave valuables at home."

There was an uneasy silence in the room after Mrs. Williams left. No one said anything. Claudine and Debbie finished getting changed and got up to leave.

"You know, someone left the gym during practice today," Sarah said, blocking the door.

"Yeah, I went to the bathroom," Debbie admitted. "So what?"

"I'm just saying," Sarah said, raising her arms and shrugging. "You had opportunity."

"This isn't a detective show, Sarah," Claudine told her. "Debbie didn't take anything."

"I'm just saying. Debbie also was the only one in the room when Nicole showed her the stuffed zebra. It's just suspicious, that's all."

She was blaming her! Debbie thought, stunned. "I didn't take anything!"

"No one says you did, Deb," Claudine told her, putting a hand on her shoulder. Debbie shook her off.

"She is! She thinks I took those things! Do you?" she asked, pointing a finger at Nicole.

She shrugged uncertainly. "I don't know you very well, Debbie," Nicole said. "I don't think you would. But where did it go?"

"I didn't take anything! Man! I don't believe this! I'm not a thief!" She said again and slammed out of the room. Claudine ran after her, calling to her to wait, but Debbie ignored her.

She let herself into the house to the tinkling sounds of "Mary had a Little Lamb" and ran up to her room, throwing herself across the bed. She lay there, face down, shoes still on, coat still on, her throat tight, her eyes stinging. They thought she was a thief! Just because she had gone to the bathroom? Who would believe she was innocent? Claudine said she did, but Debbie didn't think the others did. Or at least, they weren't sure. And what about Mrs. Williams and Mr. Anderson? Why would they believe her when she said she hadn't done anything? No one ever had before.

There were footsteps on the stairs and a tap on the door. "Deb? Everything okay?"

"Go away," Debbie said into the comforter.

"Won't you tell me what happened?" Angie asked, coming into the room. There was a creak and Debbie felt the mattress shift as she sat down.

"Nothing happened. I'm just tired. Leave me alone."

"Well, fine, then," Angie said, sounding hurt. She got off the bed and left the room. After a while, Debbie got up and kicked off her shoes. She should have known something like this would happen. She would always be the stupid foster kid, the one to blame when things happened. It didn't matter that she had a beautiful new bedroom and new clothes. It didn't matter that she lived with a mom and dad instead of foster parents. It hadn't really changed anything.

13

Defense

B ut I wasn't doing anything!" Debbie cried, looking in disbelief at the supervisor, who stood frowning before her, one hand on her hip, the other waving a clipboard in the air.

"Didn't you just spend a week in lunch detention for throwing snowballs?" the woman asked.

"Yes, but," Debbie began, but the supervisor cut her off.

"No, no buts. You have snow in your hand, Debbie, in the shape of a ball. What am I supposed to think?"

"You could let me explain," Debbie muttered. She had been planning to throw it, but only at the tree! Not that this woman cared about the truth.

"I don't want to hear the excuses, Debbie. You are not to pick snow up at all. Got it? Mr. Vanelli warned you that he wouldn't let you play basketball if you got caught again, doesn't that mean anything to you?"

Debbie scuffed at a small mound of dirty snow, scowling. She had forgotten that, actually. She just wanted to practice throwing. Greg had said she could sign up for softball in the spring and she didn't want to look like a complete fool on the field.

"Go and find something else to do, and don't let me catch you with snow in your hand again, understand?" the supervisor said, flashing a small smile.

Debbie grinned and took off before the supervisor changed her mind. The game that afternoon was against the Devils and

Mr. Anderson had told them they all had to play their best because the Devils were tough. He wouldn't have been impressed if Debbie had been pulled. She would have to be more careful. Especially since she'd gotten into a screaming match with another supervisor the day before when she'd been caught climbing over the fence. It didn't matter that she had been retrieving a ball for some little kid. This school was worse than her old one with their dumb rules.

* * *

The game was not going well for the Stars. By halftime they were already trailing by ten points. They sat on the bench, shoulders hunched, already defeated. Mr. Anderson walked back and forth in front of them, clapping his hands, punching the air to make a point.

"You are just as good as any team in this league," he told them. "Don't let a little set-back throw you off. You have to fight until the final whistle. We aren't out of this game yet, but we do have to fight hard to get back in it. Guard your players tighter. Don't let them get away from you and if they do, race back and cut them off again before the basket. Use your arms! Use your hips!"

The whistle blew and the girls stood up. Mr. Anderson quickly named the girls he wanted on the floor and the rest sat down again. Debbie was not having a good game. She had a lot of personal fouls already and had almost come to blows with a Devils player when she'd been tripped. Her mind wasn't fully on the game, she knew. She couldn't help wondering if the other girls were looking at her, thinking "thief!"

To make matters more complicated, she was having a heck of a time with a guard from the Devils, some girl named Trish. She had long arms and legs and a long face that seemed always to be right in Debbie's. She was driving Debbie nuts, cutting off the lane when she tried to drive, or shoving at her, throwing her off balance. Trish was doing her job so well that Debbie had been held to only six points so far.

Sarah missed the lay-up and the Devils raced up court. Trish threw up a bad shot from the corner and the ball bounced off the rim, right in to the waiting hands of Claudine. Debbie, seeing a possible fast break, turned and raced toward the Stars' basket. Unfortunately Claudine's pass was short and Debbie had to slow down so she could catch it. As she spun to shoot, Trish was there, blocking her. As Debbie jumped up, off balance, the two girls collided. Trish made a big production of falling backwards, arms waving in the air wildly. Debbie shook her head, looking in disgust at the little performance. Unfortunately, the ref called the foul on Debbie anyway putting their team over their foul limit and sending Trish to the free throw.

"What! She was acting! Anyone could see she was acting. Her feet weren't set and I didn't hit her that hard!"

But nothing that Debbie said changed the ref's mind. Mr. Anderson sent Nicole in for Debbie and she headed to the bench, furious.

"Let it go, Deb," Mr. Anderson told her. "Sometimes it happens. Don't let it throw your game."

In the end, however, despite the Stars' best efforts, the Devils beat them thirty-eight to thirty-one. The mood in the changing room was not a pleasant one. Sarah, mad at spending a lot of the game on the bench, threw things around, making everyone around her angry. Debbie, still upset at the lousy call and her own poor performance, was very quiet. She took off her shoes slowly, keeping her face down. She reached into her bag, pulling it open. As she did so, a pretty silver key chain fell out of the bag. She stared at it in surprise.

"My key chain!" Sarah cried, pouncing on it. "What are you doing with it? You must have taken it from my bag!"

"I don't know how it got in my bag!" Debbie said. Her hands were shaking and she had to put her bag down. "Someone must have planted it there."

"Yeah right, Debbie! I knew it was you! You come in here all full of yourself because your dad is a coach, but you're nothing but a thief! I think you should be kicked off the team!"

Debbie looked around at the other girls. Some were sympathetic, like Claudine, but most were unsure. Nicole wouldn't meet her eyes at all. "I didn't take anything!" Debbie didn't bother to finish changing, just grabbed her things and ran from the room.

At dinner that night Debbie was very quiet. She found it hard to eat, even though it was a stir fry, which she loved. She poked at the food on her plate, wanting to go back to her room. She knew it was pointless to ask. Angie was very strict about table manners. You stayed at the table until everyone was finished, even if you didn't feel like eating yourself.

"Something bothering you, Deb?" Greg asked gently.

Debbie shook her head. Why bother saying anything? Eventually they'd find out anyway and probably send her back. She didn't want to hurt them before it was necessary.

"You've been kind of mopey for a few days. You know you can talk to us about anything. We'll try to help."

Tears sprang to Debbie's eyes and she wiped at them furiously. She wouldn't cry about it! "There isn't anything to tell."

"Is it the loss today? Paige told me you had a rough time against the Devils," Greg said. "She thought there were some bad calls made."

"There were. The ref was lousy."

"Sometimes that happens. It's best to just let it go. Try again the next time. Don't you play the Eagles next week? I've heard they are pretty slow. Sounds like an easy win for you guys."

Debbie let Greg talk. If he believed she was upset about losing the game that day, he wouldn't try and get anything more out of her. Finally everyone finished eating and Debbie could escape to her room. She turned the stereo on, louder than usual, and sat at her desk, staring at the photo of Jenna. When Greg and Angie sent her back, would she go back to Darlene and Steve? she wondered. That would be okay. At least then she could be with Jenna.

* * *

Debbie had known that Sarah wouldn't let the key chain thing rest and sure enough she was called to Mr. Vanelli's office at the end of the following day. Greg and Angie were there too, sitting side by side, their faces serious but not angry. They smiled when she came in and sat down in the third chair.

Mr. Vanelli got straight to the point. "Sarah Percy has made a very serious accusation," he said. "She claims her key chain was found in your bag yesterday, Debbie. She also says a number of other things have gone missing from the change room and that you had opportunity to take them."

"I didn't take anything," Debbie said, staring at the worn carpet.

"We don't take stealing lightly in this school," the principal said sternly.

"I'm sure you don't, Mr. Vanelli," Angie said slowly. "But perhaps we could hear Debbie's side of things."

"No one is going to believe me anyway."

"Why don't you just tell us what happened and then we'll go from there," Greg suggested, squeezing her arm.

"Nicole showed me the stuffed zebra before practice last week or whenever it was. Then she put it in her bag."

"You were the only one in the room?" Angie asked. "Did anyone else come in, or leave practice even for a minute that day?"

"Sarah poked her head in real quick to tell us to hurry up, that Mrs. Williams was waiting," Debbie remembered. "And I think Stephanie went to the bathroom."

"What about Claudine's wallet? What happened that day?"

"Well, I never saw the wallet. I mean, I knew she had it, but I never saw it in the changing room. I went to the bathroom during practice but I used the hall one, not the one in the changing room. And at yesterday's game, I never left the gym. I don't know how the key chain got in my bag, but I didn't put it there."

"It does look very suspicious, though, Debbie," Mr. Vanelli said, tapping his fingers against his chin. Debbie squeezed her hands between her knees. She hadn't thought he would believe her.

"It does look suspicious, but Debbie says she didn't take anything and she wouldn't lie to us," Angie said.

"I think there is room for doubt here. Anyone could have planted that key chain in her bag." Greg added.

They believed her? She looked at Greg and Angie, frowning. They looked back at her, smiling. "You believe me?" she asked.

"Of course we believe you. We've asked you if you know anything about the missing things and you have said no. Are you telling us the truth?"

"Yes. I'm not a thief."

"Exactly. So, Mr. Vanelli," Greg said, "I think there needs to be some more investigating."

"Yes, there does," the principal agreed.

* * *

Debbie walked home between Greg and Angie. She felt as though she had walked a very long way. She could lie down right there in the road and go to sleep. No one said anything until they were alone in the house and Poker had been properly greeted.

"Come in here a second, Deb," Greg said, going into the family room. He and Angie sat down on the couch and invited Debbie to join them.

She sat down warily. There had been talk in Mr. Vanelli's office about the trouble Debbie had been getting into on the playground and in class. She had promised to try harder to control her temper but if she didn't both Greg and Angie had agreed with Mr. Vanelli that Debbie would have to be supervised during recess and lunch. There had been no yelling or threats in the office but were they going to yell now that they were home?

"I'm wondering why you didn't tell us about the stealing business," Greg began. "Did you think we wouldn't believe you?"

Debbie shrugged. "Have we done something to make you think we wouldn't believe you?" Angie asked.

"I don't know. No one ever believed me before. Darlene always figured I was to blame. So did everyone at the school." She looked up to catch Greg and Angie exchanging glances.

"We aren't Darlene. And we certainly aren't the people at your old school. If you tell us something, we believe it's true."

"Does all this have something to do with the suitcases I found in your closet this morning?" Angie asked gently. "I put some clothes away for you and found them."

Debbie stared hard over Angie's shoulder, out into the yard still spotty with snow and little brown mounds of dog poop. What was she supposed to say?

"You know you can't go back to Darlene and Steve, right?" Angie asked. "You understand that you are our daughter now, for ever and ever? If we move away from this house, you will come with us. If you get in trouble at school, suspended even, we will still be your parents. Nothing that you can do or say will change our minds about that."

Debbie stared down at her hands folded in her lap. She swallowed hard.

"Look at me, Deb, please," Greg asked gently. Debbie looked up reluctantly, meeting his eyes.

"Angie and I are your parents now. We are your mom and dad. We love you."

A long silence filled the room. No one had ever, ever told Debbie they loved her before. Maybe her mom had, years ago, but Debbie didn't remember that. It felt strange and a little frightening, really. But then, parents did love their children, she told herself. Jenna's mom and dad loved Jenna and her sister, Carlie. They were always hugging and kissing them both and calling them silly names. And Jenna and Carlie loved their parents.

"How do you know you love me?" Debbie asked. "I mean, you haven't known me very long."

Greg ran a hand over his beard, pulling on his chin. "Well," he said slowly, "I guess it doesn't have to take very long with some people. With people who are right for each other."

"But how do you know?"

"I feel it, Deb, in my heart. I think I knew I would love you when we met you in the restaurant. Remember? You were so worried, frowning at everyone, wondering what was going on, who we were. I said to myself right then, I want this girl to be my daughter. Angie felt the same way. And then, as we got to know you over the next weeks, I just knew it more."

"Maybe you just wanted a kid so bad you tricked yourself," Debbie said, turning to look at Angie.

Angie smiled, but shook her head. "Perhaps at first, when I was so excited that we'd finally found a child who we thought would fit with our family, but once I met you I just knew you were the little girl we had been waiting for for so long. And everything that has happened since then has only made me believe that more."

"What if you stop loving me?"

Angie reached out and took hold of Debbie's hands. She held them tightly. "That will never, ever happen."

"My real mom stopped loving me. You could too."

"Your birth mother has never stopped loving you, Deb. Not once, ever. And neither will we. I understand you find that hard to believe right now, but that's okay. It won't change how I feel, or how Greg feels." Angie bent over and kissed Debbie's forehead, pressing her lips against the skin for a long second.

"We are a family, Debbie. You can tell us anything and we will listen and help you as much as we can. No matter what you do or say we will always love you and care for you. That's the way it is."

14

The Plan

W hy didn't you tell me?" Paige demanded. "I would have popped that stupid old Sarah Percy right in the nose."

"Then you would have been in trouble," Debbie told her.

"And besides," Claudine added, "Sarah is bigger than you. She'd cream you if you tried to fight her."

The three girls were locked in Paige's room. Practice that afternoon had been a tense, strained affair with Sarah throwing Debbie dirty looks the whole time, trying to trip her, making rude comments about thieves. Still, Debbie had done her best to ignore her. She had promised Greg and Angie that she would work hard at controlling her temper and staying out of trouble and she meant to keep her word, if she could.

"So Mr. Vanelli believed you then?" Claudine asked, finishing the last of her cupcake. She brushed the chocolate crumbs off her shirt and lay back on the bed.

"Yeah."

"Is he going to try and figure out who the real thief is?" Paige asked.

"I don't know if he is or not. But I'm not waiting around till he does. I think we should try and figure it out ourselves," Debbie announced. She had been thinking about it since the night before. Why couldn't she and Claudine and Paige be detectives and catch the real thief?

"How are we supposed to do that?" Claudine sat up, frowning at Debbie. "I mean, I'm not a detective. I can't even solve those Encyclopedia Brown books and they're so easy."

"Well, we'll have to figure that out," Debbie told them. "We'll have to set the thief up. Do either of you have a tape recorder?" she asked. Both girls shook their heads.

"Scott used to belong to some kind of club for amateur detectives," Paige suddenly remembered. "Maybe he still has some of that old stuff. Should I go look?"

"Won't he get mad if you go in his room?" Claudine asked but Paige didn't look concerned.

"Why would he know? I'll be back in a sec."

She came back waving a black box. Carefully they opened it on the bed and looked at the contents. There was a magnifying glass that made Paige's eye look huge when she held it up to her face, and a fingerprint dusting kit. Claudine grabbed at it, but frowned when she realized all the powder had been used. There was a little notebook and a yellow pencil and a small bottle with an orange gel-like substance in it.

"What's that?" Claudine asked as Debbie picked up the bottle. She read the label.

"It says it's skin dye. 'Catch any crook "red" handed with Dr. Doom's miracle skin dye. Guaranteed to expose any light-fingered thief.' This," Debbie said, waving the bottle at her friends, "is just what we were looking for."

* * *

It was hard not to look at each other and giggle all through the following Monday, but the girls kept their cool. Since they didn't know who the real thief was, they weren't taking any chances that it was someone in their own classroom. For all they knew, the theif might be sitting next to one of them, so it wouldn't do to raise suspicion.

Finally the bell rang and Debbie and Claudine rushed out the door to the changing room. The other girls slowly trickled in. When everyone was in the room, Claudine cleared her throat nervously, then opened the bag hanging from a hook on the wall.

"Did I show you the new Tigger I got over the weekend?" she asked Debbie, just loud enough that everyone could hear her. "He's a limited edition one."

Debbie looked in the bag at the small orange and gray creature lying on the top of Claudine's clothes. "He's cute. I'd love to have one. I'd love to have the whole set."

"Yeah. But they're kind of expensive. I had to save my allowance for weeks." She closed the top of the bag and hung it up again. They kept talking a little more quietly about the stuffed toy until they were the only ones left in the room.

"Do you think whoever it is will try and take it?" Debbie asked Claudine as they left the room together.

"I guess we'll find out in an hour," Claudine said.

"What if the stuff doesn't work?"

"It worked on Paige when we tried it, right?" Claudine reminded her. "Relax. It'll work."

They didn't get to find out if it worked that day because when they returned to the changing room after practice and Claudine opened her bag, Tigger was still lying there. Her shoulders fell slightly and she glanced at Debbie. They didn't say anything until they were safe in Debbie's bedroom fifteen minutes later. Paige slumped into the chair at the desk and pouted.

"Now what?" she asked.

"We just keep trying," Debbie told her. "We have to figure out who did it or the girls will never believe it wasn't me. Maybe we talked about it too much. Maybe next time you should let it fall out of your bag or something and just be careful to lift it by the tail so you don't get the stuff on your own fingers."

"Did you see anyone leave practice, Paige?" Claudine asked, her dark eyes anxious. "I kept trying to look at the door, but it was hard with all the running we had to do."

"Yeah, two girls got a drink of water, but no one went in the changing room."

"You didn't let them see you, did you?" Debbie asked, alarmed. If the thief thought someone was patrolling, she would never try and take the tiger.

"No," Paige said scornfully. "What do you think I am, stupid? I hid around the corner. You couldn't see me coming or going from the gym."

"Well, I guess we just have to wait until Wednesday now."

After lunch on Wednesday Debbie realized she hadn't brought her gym strip back to school after taking it home to be washed on Monday. Mr. Anderson agreed to let her run home and get it and as soon as the bell rang at two thirty, she bolted out of the class and home. It took her a couple of minutes to find her shorts and she could hear the thud of balls and the squeak of sneakers on the gym floor as she made her way to the changing room. She waved to Paige, hiding in the shadows, then pulled open the door.

Sarah was still in the room, tucking something in her bag as Debbie came in. The two girls ignored each other. Debbie found a spot on the bench and sat down to change her clothes. Sarah closed the zipper on her bag then turned. As she passed Debbie, she lifted her arms up, a hair elastic in one hand. Debbie caught the glint of colour as the overhead lights hit Sarah's hand. She gasped. Sarah's right hand was orange!

"You!" Debbie cried. "You were the one all along!" In a second Paige was in the room too, reacting to Debbie's voice.

Sarah scowled at the two girls and went to push past. "I don't know what you're talking about," she muttered. "Let me go!"

Debbie grabbed Sarah's hand and forced her to turn it over. Sarah looked down and her eyes widened in surprise at the colour. "Go get Mrs. Williams," Debbie told Paige, hanging on tightly to Sarah. The other girl tried to pull her hand away but Debbie held tightly.

"I can't believe you would set me up like that. What did I ever do to you?" she asked.

"You think you're so great, with your new parents and your dad being a coach. Always acting like such a hot shot. Thinking you're better than everyone else."

"I don't think I'm better than everyone else and I can't help it if my dad is a coach!" The words came out of her mouth as though she said them all the time: My dad. It felt good, and right, somehow, and she smiled to herself. And if Greg was her dad, well then, that made Angie her mom.

The conversation she'd had with them both the other night came back to her: "Angie and I are your parents now. We are your mom and dad. We love you," Greg had said. A tingle ran up Debbie's back. She was part of a real and forever family, and Sarah was jealous.

Sarah's face darkened even more and she tried again to wrench free of Debbie's grip on her arm. "My dad, my dad, my dad! God! That's all you say all the time! Why don't you just shut up about your dumb parents for once!" Sarah cried, her orange fingers clenched in fists. "You can keep your stupid parents. You'll see, they'll be just as bad as your foster parents were."

"You could be adopted one day, Sarah," Debbie said gently. "I mean, I never thought I would be and it happened."

Sarah made a rude noise and scowled harder. Her eyes were shiny and her voice caught as she spoke. "I can't be adopted, not ever. My mom won't let me be."

Before Debbie could answer, the door banged open and Mrs. Williams and most of the team crowded into the tiny changing room. Debbie stepped back, away from the crowd, while Claudine and Paige explained what they had done and showed the teacher Sarah's orange fingers.

"It was from my brother Scott's old detective kit," Paige began.

"We tried it on Monday but nothing happened," Claudine said.

"It was Debbie's idea. She wanted to clear her name."

"It's skin dye. Look," Claudine said, pulling out the small bottle. "It doesn't show up on cloth or fabric, only on human skin. But don't worry, Sarah," she said, narrowing her eyes at the girl, "you're hand won't fall off. It isn't toxic."

"It'll wear off in a couple of hours," Paige explained.

"Come with me, Sarah," Mrs. Williams said and left the room, Sarah following sullenly behind.

"The rest of you get back to practice," Mr. Anderson said, herding them all back into the gym. Claudine and Paige looked at Debbie and grinned. Debbie tried to smile, but she couldn't help glancing down the hallway toward Mr. Vanelli's office. She hoped they weren't too hard on Sarah.

* * *

"And so the real reason Sarah hated me was because she has been a foster kid for years and can't be adopted. Her birth mom won't give up her rights, or something like that," Debbie told Greg and Angie that night at dinner. It still seemed rather unbelievable to Debbie.

"How sad," Angie said from across the table.

Debbie chewed thoughtfully for a few minutes, thinking. "She's a lot like me, isn't she?" she said finally. "I mean, kind of mad at everyone and stuff? Plus she's been moved four times! At least I only had two foster homes before I came here. I always thought it would be better if I could see my mom, but Sarah sees hers all the time and she doesn't seem very happy."

"No. I'm sure she isn't. It must be very hard for her," Greg agreed.

"You know, Deb," Angie said, "I'm very proud of the way you solved the problem and stood up for yourself. And I'm proud of the way you've been trying so hard at school to control your anger. Mr. Anderson called today to tell us that you'd been doing a good job since our meeting last week."

Debbie blushed. He'd said the same thing to her that very day. And most of the girls on the team had come up to her and apologized for not believing her when she'd said she hadn't taken anything. Scott had offered to teach her some new moves on the basketball court and Paige had invited her for a sleep over that weekend. Life looked pretty close to perfect. Poker rubbed up against her leg, looking for scraps and she slipped him a small piece of chicken.

"Don't feed the dog from the table," Greg told her. "Poker, get out of the kitchen."

Poker slunk away to his mat, tail between his legs, his eyes sad. Debbie laughed. "It's okay, Poke," she reassured him. "I'll save you a little bit for later."

She looked at Angie and then over at Greg. They were discussing something that had happened to Greg at work that day. Angie laughed, holding a hand to her throat. These were her parents, Debbie told herself again. This was her family. She felt a thickening in her throat and a twinge in her chest. She looked around her at the bright yellow kitchen with the plants and the collection of watering cans and then down into the family room where Poker lay in his basket. He thumped his tail at her and she smiled. The twinge came again and she realized what it was. The pain in her chest wasn't a heart attack or indigestion, it was love.

Was this what Greg had been talking about the other night? This funny ache? It seemed strange to Debbie, strange and a little overwhelming. But then, kids did love their parents, didn't they? And they called their parents Mom and Dad, too. Well, she would start practising, in her head, and maybe, soon ...

"I thought we might watch a bit of that basketball game on TV tonight," Greg said, wiping at his mouth with a serviette.

"Sounds great," Debbie told him, welcoming the strange but wonderful pain inside her, "but first I have some unpacking to do."

Other books you'll enjoy in the Sports Stories series ...

Baseball

☐ *Curve Ball* by John Danakas #1
Tom Poulos is looking forward to a summer of baseball in Toronto until his mother puts him on a plane to Winnipeg.

☐ *Baseball Crazy* by Martyn Godfrey #10
Rob Carter wins an all-expenses-paid chance to be bat boy at the Blue Jays spring training camp in Florida.

☐ *Shark Attack* by Judi Peers #25
The East City Sharks have a good chance of winning the county championship until their arch rivals get a tough new pitcher.

☐ *Hit and Run* by Dawn Hunter and Karen Hunter #35
Glen Thomson is a talented pitcher, but as his ego inflates, team morale plummets. Will he learn from being benched for losing his temper?

☐ *Power Hitter* by C. A. Forsyth #41
Connor's summer was looking like a write-off. That is, until he discovered his secret talent.

☐ *Sayonara, Sharks* by Judi Peers #48
Ben and Kate are excited about the school trip to Japan, but Matt's not sure he wants to go.

Basketball

☐ *Fast Break* by Michael Coldwell #8
Moving from Toronto to small-town Nova Scotia was rough, but when Jeff makes the school basketball team he thinks things are looking up.

☐ *Camp All-Star* by Michael Coldwell #12
In this insider's view of a basketball camp, Jeff Lang encounters some unexpected challenges.

☐ *Nothing but Net* by Michael Coldwell #18
The Cape Breton Grizzly Bears prepare for an out-of-town basketball tournament they're sure to lose.

☐ *Slam Dunk* by Steven Barwin and Gabriel David Tick #23
In this sequel to *Roller Hockey Blues*, Mason Ashbury's basketball team adjusts to the arrival of some new players: girls.

☐ *Courage on the Line* by Cynthia Bates #33
After Amelie changes schools, she must confront difficult former teammates in an extramural match.

☐ *Free Throw* by Jacqueline Guest #34
Matthew Eagletail must adjust to a new school, a new team and a new father along with five pesky sisters.

☐ *Triple Threat* by Jacqueline Guest #38
Matthew's cyber-pal Free Throw comes to visit, and together they face a bully on the court.

☐ *Queen of the Court* by Michele Martin Bossley #40
What happens when the school's fashion queen winds up on the basketball court?

☐ *Shooting Star* by Cynthia Bates #46
Quyen is dealing with a troublesome teammate on her new basketball team, as well as trouble at home. Her parents seem haunted by something that happened in Vietnam.

☐ *Home Court Advantage* by Sandra Diersch #51
Debbie had given up hope of being adopted, until the Lowells came along. Adoption means moving, and making the basketball team at her new school helps. That is, until Debbie is accused of stealing from the team.

Figure Skating

☐ *A Stroke of Luck* by Kathryn Ellis #6
Strange accidents are stalking one of the skaters at the Millwood Arena.

☐ *The Winning Edge* by Michele Martin Bossley #28
Jennie wants more than anything to win a gruelling series of competitions, but is success worth losing her friends?

☐ *Leap of Faith* by Michele Martin Bossley #36
Amy wants to win at any cost, until an injury makes skating almost impossible. Will she go on?

Gymnastics

☐ *The Perfect Gymnast* by Michele Martin Bossley #9
Abby's new friend has all the confidence she needs, but she also has a serious problem that nobody but Abby seems to know about.

Ice Hockey

☐ *Two Minutes for Roughing* by Joseph Romain #2
As a new player on a tough Toronto hockey team, Les must fight to fit in.

☐ *Hockey Night in Transcona* by John Danakas #7
Cody Powell gets promoted to the Transcona Sharks' first line, bumping out the coach's son, who's not happy with the change.

☐ *Face Off* by C. A. Forsyth #13
A talented hockey player finds himself competing with his best friend for a spot on a select team.

☐ *Hat Trick* by Jacqueline Guest #20
The only girl on an all-boy hockey team works to earn the captain's respect and her mother's approval.

☐ *Hockey Heroes* by John Danakas #22
A left-winger on the thirteen-year-old Transcona Sharks adjusts to a new best friend and his mom's boyfriend.

☐ *Hockey Heat Wave* by C. A. Forsyth #27
In this sequel to *Face Off*, Zack and Mitch run into trouble when it looks as if only one of them will make the select team at hockey camp.

☐ *Shoot to Score* by Sandra Richmond #31
Playing defense on the B list alongside the coach's mean-spirited son is a tough obstacle for Steven to overcome, but he perseveres and changes his luck.

☐ *Rookie Season* by Jacqueline Guest #42
What happens when a boy wants to join an all-girl hockey team?

☐ *Brothers on Ice* by John Danakas #44
Brothers Dylan and Deke both want to play goal for the same team.

☐ *Rink Rivals* by Jacqueline Guest #49
A move to Calgary finds the Evans twins pitted against each other on the ice, and struggling to help each other out of trouble.

☐ *Power Play* by Michele Martin Bossley #50
An early-season injury causes Zach Thomas to play timidly, and a school bully is just making matters worse. Zach hopes a famous hockey player will be able to help him sort things out.

Riding

☐ *A Way with Horses* by Peter McPhee #11
A young Alberta rider, invited to study show jumping at a posh local riding school, uncovers a secret.

☐ *Riding Scared* by Marion Crook #15
A reluctant new rider struggles to overcome her fear of horses.

☐ *Katie's Midnight Ride* by C. A. Forsyth #16
An ambitious barrel racer finds herself without a horse weeks before her biggest rodeo.

☐ *Glory Ride* by Tamara L. Williams #21
Chloe Anderson fights memories of a tragic fall for a place on the Ontario Young Riders Team.

☐ *Cutting It Close* by Marion Crook #24
In this novel about barrel racing, a young rider finds her horse is in trouble just as she's about to compete in an important event.

☐ *Shadow Ride* by Tamara L. Williams #37
Bronwen has to choose between competing aggressively for herself or helping out a teammate.

Roller Hockey

☐ Roller Hockey Blues by Steven Barwin and Gabriel David Tick #17
Mason Ashbury faces a summer of boredom until he makes the roller hockey team.

Running

☐ *Fast Finish* by Bill Swan #30
Noah is a promising young runner headed for the provincial finals when he suddenly decides to withdraw from the event.

Sailing

☐ *Sink or Swim* by William Pasnak #5
Dario can barely manage the dog paddle, but thanks to his mother he's spending the summer at a water sports camp.

Soccer

☐ *Lizzie's Soccer Showdown* by John Danakas #3
When Lizzie asks why the boys and girls can't play together, she finds herself the new captain of the soccer team.

☐ *Alecia's Challenge* by Sandra Diersch #32
Thirteen-year-old Alecia has to cope with a new school, a new step-father and friends who have suddenly discovered the opposite sex.

☐ *Shut-Out!* by Camilla Reghelini Rivers #39
David wants to play soccer more than anything, but will the new coach let him?

☐ *Offside!* by Sandra Diersch #43
Alecia has to confront a new girl who drives her teammates crazy.

☐ *Heads Up!* by Dawn Hunter and Karen Hunter #45
Do the Warriors really need a new, hot-shot player who skips practice?

☐ *Off the Wall* by Camilla Reghelini Rivers #52
The only bright spot in Lizzie's life is indoor soccer, and she's thrilled when her little sister gets into the sport. But when their teams are pitted against each other, Lizzie can only warn her sister to watch out.

Swimming

☐ *Breathing Not Required* by Michele Martin Bossley #4
Gracie works so hard to be chosen for the solo at synchronized swimming that she almost loses her best friend in the process.

☐ *Water Fight!* by Michele Martin Bossley #14
Josie's perfect sister is driving her crazy, but when she takes up swimming — Josie's sport — it's too much to take.

☐ *Taking a Dive* by Michele Martin Bossley #19
Josie holds the provincial record for the butterfly, but in this sequel to *Water Fight!*, she can't seem to match her own time and might not go on to the nationals.

☐ *Great Lengths* by Sandra Diersch #26
Fourteen-year-old Jessie decides to find out whether the rumours about a new swimmer at her Vancouver club are true.

☐ *Pool Princess* by Michele Martin Bossley #47
In this sequel to *Breathing Not Required*, Gracie must deal with a bully on the new synchro team that she joins in Calgary.

Track and Field

☐ *Mikayla's Victory* by Cynthia Bates #29
Mikayla must compete against her friend if she wants to represent her school at an important track event.